To CAJ

Bob Berg

CW00695412

Love takes you home

Pino cooks to keep his memory of home alive. He sniffs and sings and moves with passion.

Valda thanks God for food and eats with gusto. She is fat and waddles as she walks.

Graziella cannot eat. She cannot digest—food or life.

And through it all Grace travels. She travels away from her family to find her home.

This is a book to savour. A generous and graceful novel about truth, taste and everyone's need to belong.

Julie Capaldo loves good food and good stories. She lives in Melbourne with her husband, three children, dog, goldfish, and a nosy neighbour who keeps popping in.

Her children will tell you she can't cook—but only writes like she can. Don't believe them—it's just that she prefers writing to cooking.

Her dream is to have a full-time, live-in Italian chef.

Love takes you home is her first novel.

Julie Capaldo

Love takes you home

A novel in 13 delicious meals

Mandarin

A Mandarin Paperback
LOVE TAKES YOU HOME

First published in Great Britain 1996
by Mandarin Paperbacks
an imprint of Reed International Books Ltd
Michelin House, 81 Fulham Road, London SW3 6RB
and Auckland, Melbourne, Singapore and Toronto

Copyright © Julie Capaldo 1995
The author has asserted her moral rights

A CIP catalogue record for this title
is available from the British Library
ISBN 0 7493 2269 1

All characters and events in this book
are fictitious and any resemblance to
real organisations or real persons,
living or dead, is purely coincidental.

Printed and bound in Great Britain by
BPC Paperbacks Ltd
a member of The British Printing Company Ltd

This book is sold subject to the condition
that it shall not, by way of trade or otherwise,
be lent, resold, hired out, or otherwise circulated
without the publisher's prior consent in any form
of binding or cover other than that in which
it is published and without a similar condition
including this condition being imposed
on the subsequent purchaser.

Chapters

Acknowledgements

Many people have helped me in my journey to create this book:

—Judy Duffy and the RMIT TAFE School of Professional Writing where, as well as professional support, I found good friends;

—Reed Books, particularly Adrian Collette and Jennifer Byrne, and freelance editor Cathy Smith, for their enthusiasm and support;

—Anita for correcting my Italian;

—my family the Capaldos, Zocchis, Piovesans, Sheridans, Willies, Mattiazzos, Lovetts, and Dohertys, who are always there for me;

—my mum Mary and my second mum Bianca for their recipes;

—my three best friends, James, Amber and Luke for eating take-away food, while I wrote about delicious meals; and

—Mark, for always believing I could do it.

1   To remember home — Pigeon in a pan

he suitcase is old. I can't tell what colour it originally was because the checked pattern on the sides has faded so much. The handle is leather and curves like a small banana; the clasps are rusted and stick. As a child, I often sneaked out to the shed and touched the suitcase, like it was a magic talisman, ran my fingers along its bumpy skin feeling for its secrets. The dusty smell of it made me cry for a land I hadn't seen, a language I couldn't speak, a person I couldn't be.

He told me the story of the suitcase many times when I was a child. And now as an adult, when I come to say goodbye, he offers it to me. His wife, Zia Valda, laughs her donkey, *hee hee hee*, laugh. 'Oh God,' she calls aloud, rolling her eyes towards the heavens and shaking her joined palms, '*Madonna mia,* tell this *stupido* man she doesn't want that old thing.' But he knows better, and when he gives me the suitcase I cannot speak. I know if the tears start they will never stop and so I silently nod and grasp it tightly. Later, when I open it to pack, I find a spiral foolscap note

3

book filled with flourishing writing, loops and swirls that dance across the paper. 'Recipes From Home', it says at the top of the page. An envelope falls from the book. It is addressed to me.

Bellisima,

I give this as a surprise to you. Many years ago I think to write my favourite recipes in this book. They are not the most spectacular, or even the most delicious, but they are the ones I love to cook best of all. When I cook them I remember who I am and where I come from. I give them to you—on loan. You know, it is not the custom of Italians to take loans, we don't like to be in debt to anyone, but this is with you for luck and safe-keeping. Maybe it will remind you of your home and family while you are away from us. Bella, one day, when I am gone, you give this to my grandchildren so they too will remember where they came from and who they are.

Tanti baci,
Zio Pino

I hug the book to me and as I feel my heart beating against it, I imagine that it is really the book's heart—pulsing into me.

When I start to pack I realise his suitcase is not big enough. I get out the travel set my parents gave me for Christmas: a large case and two bags in a matching tapestry weave. The clasps are shiny and click open with precision. Inside, the case has mesh inserts— for holding shoes, I suppose. The smaller bag is for hand luggage and has so many zips and flaps that I am scared off immediately. I can just see myself in the airport terminal fumbling through all the compartments for my ticket. The third bag is oval shaped like a hat box. It is a make-up bag. I never wear make-up so the bag seems particularly useless and out of place—I know exactly how it feels.

I sniff the three bags. A short blast of plastic and chemicals fills my head. I sniff the old suitcase Zio Pino gave me and the smell lingers and is warm inside me. It reminds me of the story he has told me so often. He left his home, his family, everything that was familiar, and all he took with him was a suitcase.

The Pit of the Abyss

He left home when he was still a boy, only seventeen, but with enough memories for a lifetime. He had grown up surrounded by rich earth that provided all his food. He had wakened to sunrises that lit the sky as suddenly as the flame of a striking match. He had listened to old men who sat in the village square and sang songs as old as the mountain. The mountain. Always, he turned and it was there—like God.

He left home when he was still a boy because he had seen all these things and more—things no man should ever see. Men shot in the back and heaved like sacks of potatoes into a deep cavern the villagers called the Pit of the Abyss. He had seen women beaten until they fell, the life sucked from them. He had seen boys put on uniforms and forget their own mothers. He left home when he was still a boy because his father was wise and wanted him to have the chance to become a man.

His father, Old Giuseppino, lived in the mountains all his life, as had his father and his father's father. When Old Giuseppino finally had a son he thought it would be the same for him. It was not. The communists had come and then the fascists, then the nationalists and then the liberationists. Or had the fascists come first then the communists? Old Giuseppino confused them all. He used to say, 'My work is my politics, my family is my religion. That is all a man need know of politics and religion.' Old Giuseppino had been called 'Old' all his life. In his family each generation named their first son Giuseppino. The tag of 'old' or 'young' alternated. His father had been Young Giuseppino and so he had been born Old. The family had lived in the mountains for longer than anyone could remember. Old Giuseppino lived in the family house and carried on the family business of cobbling. He was traditional in all but one area. When his son was born he did not name him Giuseppino.

'Enough of the "old" and "young". A man should be allowed to be who he is without the burden of another's name,' he said. So Pino, son of Old Giuseppino, was granted the freedom to be his own man—in name. He grew into a happy child, obedient and respectful. He had the big nose of his father, and proud forehead of his grandfather. But his tastebuds were like Maria's, his mother. She loved to cook. To chop, fry, stir, sprinkle—it lightened her heart and gave her pleasure. Her son shared her pleasure. Although he was learning the family trade of being a cobbler, his hands were fine and more suited to mincing parsley and dicing onion than cutting pieces of leather and pounding on the cobbler's last. Pino worked all day with his father but when they returned home at night he watched over his mother's shoulder as she cooked, asking her about the herbs she used, and while she grated the cheese he leaned over the bubbling pot so that the steam dampened his skin and the smell seeped through his pores.

It was a tradition that on his deathbed, the cobbler's last be handed to the eldest son. That was how it was given to Old Giuseppino, and his father before him and his father before him. When the invading troops took it away from Old Giuseppino and threw it into the Pit of the Abyss he called his son aside. 'Pino, these are cowards who speak the words of another man and hide in uniforms. It is not capitalism or communism that they fight— it is life. You must leave, my son. Leave the home of our ancestors to keep your spirit alive.'

So Pino left. Riding his bicycle through the mountains at night until his legs throbbed and his chest ached. He rode until he reached the sea, and the mountains were hazy blue lumps in the background. His father had hidden some money in the handlebars, and he used it all to buy a passage on a ship leaving for Australia.

He swapped his bicycle for a suitcase—it was empty but it gave him a sense of hope. He stood on the deck of the ship, holding it. The suitcase felt light, but he knew when he arrived in the new country he would fill it with riches. Each day he stood on the deck holding his empty suitcase. Gradually, after weeks at sea, his mood changed. His grip on the handle tightened until his knuckles popped, white. As he looked out across the horizon and saw only mountains of waves and fields of water he trembled and retched. He feared he had fallen into the Pit of the Abyss.

I pack underwear and socks first. They are life's essentials after all. 'Change your underwear and socks every day,' my mother used to say. 'They are a good measure of time. When you go away for five days you pack five pairs, if you go away for two days you pack two pairs, see what I mean?' I don't know how long I'm going for so I put them all in. The suitcase is nearly full already. I wonder how essential these essentials really are? How much time do I waste with the unneccessary?

Zia Valda doesn't wear underpants. She stopped wearing undies about five years ago when she read about feminism and became, as she called it, 'a feminister'. She said it was a great way to tell if the washing would dry. 'When it feels all breezy down there,' she pointed between her legs, 'I know the clothes will dry.' Her daughter Angelina was horrified. 'Oh Ma,' she groaned as she rolled her eyes and waved her hands around, 'you are so embarrassing. Even if you don't wear knickers at least wear a roll-on! Ma, how could you do this to me?' Angelina was always moaning about something. Last time I saw her, the day she did my hair, she was still complaining.

'Jeez you don't know how lucky you are that you came from a *normal* family,' she said. She massaged my scalp with strong fingers as she shampooed my hair. 'How come you always hung around us? You were like another cousin—you know what wogs are like, everyone's a cousin. Hey, your hair feels much better now. You're looking much better too.'

I tried to get a word in, which was always a challenge when Angelina was talking. 'I liked your place,' I said. 'It was so ... so ...' I searched for the right word, 'so friendly.'

'Friendly!' Angelina slopped water on my face, it trickled down my neck. 'It was a frigging madhouse.'

She was right. It *was* a madhouse. Full of noise and music and smells. I was younger, chubby and soft, with pale blue eyes and dark curly hair. I smiled a lot when I was with them, and they let me listen in and follow them around. I thought Angelina was the most beautiful girl I had seen, with her bouffant hair and jangling earrings, and her brothers, Giuseppe, Alessandro and Russell, were so dark and handsome. Zio Pino would sit Alessandro and I on the green chair beside him and he would tell us stories. The rest of the family sat at his feet or leaned on the back of his chair, close to his head, so our legs and arms lightly touched each other. We formed a circle where the stories could spin and grow and were kept alive.

Zio Pino told us many things, about people, places, tastes and good food. 'You can tell a lot about a person by the way they eat,' he said. 'Italians have good appetites and eat with *gusto*, passion. When you see people nibble at their food, pick like a little spoggy, aaah, you know straight away that person is finicky. You know, when I first came to Australia they would not let me cook. The *Australiani* did not know how to eat good food because they did not know how to cook.'

I would ask Zio Pino what they did cook.

'Pooh!' He threw up his hands in horror. 'A bit of salt, a bit of dripping, even some ash from the cigarette. The vegetables were so slushy you could not tell if they were carrot or cabbage. And the meat! Aaah,' he shook his hands and rolled his eyes heavenwards. '*Che miseria*, it was hard, like leather. I kept a piece once and sent it to my papà to make shoes from.'

'No,' I said.

'Is true,' Zio protested. 'It made beautiful shoes but my papà said the dogs came sniffing and licking his feet every time he wore them.'

I laughed then and Zio winked at me and tousled my hair. His hand, warm on my head.

The lucky country

'Woof, woof, woof,' they said. Pino wondered if he had arrived in a nation of dogs when he heard the people of Australia speak. His ears hurt for the first month until he grew accustomed to the snapping, snarling voices. He was sent to a small country town where people stared at his fine face and called him a 'wog'. They drank a gold, bitter beer, and he yearned for the fine aroma and subtle flavour of a chianti.

During the day he picked fruit until his hands bled and his back ached. His stomach hurt and cramped from food that was greasy and tasteless and nothing he recognised. At night he lay on the narrow hard bunk in a room with thirty other men. He sniffed the warm odour of their bodies and listened to the hum of breath and snoring. There were three windows along the back wall and from there he could see the sky. Constellations that were out of place sparkled over the flat orange land that seemed to go on forever. It was not home.

Pino met Jack the cook at the orchard. Jack was a huge man, with flaming hair, a bushy beard and a cigarette permanently fixed to his bottom lip. He either didn't speak at all or yelled so loudly that the whole camp heard him. One day, when one of the men complained about the food, Jack went over and grabbed the man by the collar, lifting him right off the floor. 'Yer wanna complain?' he growled. 'I bin doin' this fer twenty years an' there's not a man alive that complains about ol' Jack's cookin'. Know what I mean?'

Pino liked to help Jack in the kitchen. The chopping and peeling had a comforting, familiar feel. Because he did whatever Jack told him to, Jack took a liking to him and taught him how to make bush stew and shepherd's pie. And while Pino was pleased of the friendship and his English improved, he never did like Jack's cooking. Jack enjoyed Pino's enthusiasm but complained about it sometimes: 'Yer make me tired just watchin' yer. Slow down. Yer a fine little worker but don't bust yer gut. The boss won't thank yer for it.' He called Pino 'Pin' because he said Pino was as sharp as a tack, although Pino didn't understand this joke for years because 'tack' made him think of *tacco*, a shoe heel.

One Saturday night Jack persuaded Pino to go to a local dance. He put on his best shirt and carefully ironed pants with sharp creases. He polished his shoes a hundred strokes each side until they were glossy mirrors, slicked back his wavy hair and brushed his teeth. He remembered his father saying, 'Pino, always have good shoes and clean teeth. It is what a woman looks for in a man.' Back home, before the soldiers had stopped the dances, he had been one of the most popular boys in the village. All the girls had hoped Pino Portelli would ask them to partner him. But this Saturday night he went home early. The girls stared and giggled when he spoke. They shook their heads as if they couldn't understand him, and no one danced with him.

On his day off he walked alongside the river and dreamed he was home and no longer a stranger with a funny accent. He sniffed and imagined he could even smell his home. *Aaah! The smell, musky and dark, but with a sweetness all its own.* He opened his eyes and looked around. He was not imagining it, something did smell familiar. He was near the old hut Jack had told him about. A hermit used to live there. A strange old fellow, Jack had said, who never spoke to anyone. People weren't sure what had happened to him, if he'd died or just moved on. Pino wandered around sniffing and then he saw what it was he was smelling—a rosemary bush half strangled in the weeds but aromatic just the same. Pino broke a piece off and put it to his nose. As he sniffed he remembered his father, his mother, her cooking. He knelt down and pulled out the weeds around the rosemary. He found sage and tarragon plants too. The area looked like it had been a herb garden. Pino carefully picked some of each and hurried back to camp. Next day, as soon as he could, he slipped away and spent the afternoon weeding and clearing the garden.

Jack was livid. He called Pino a lazy bludger and demanded to know where he had been all day. Pino didn't want to tell Jack about the garden, so he made up a story about meeting a girl. He felt ashamed for lying, sure that Jack would see through him. He looked so guilty, Jack believed the story immediately. 'Yer sly devil,' he chided. 'Gawd, and to think I thought yer were a bit slow. Go for it, Pin.'

I once asked Zio Pino what his hobbies were. What would he do when he retired? He looked at me blankly, his almond-shaped eyes blinking rapidly as if trying to see the meaning of my words. He cooked, he worked in the garden, he listened to the operas of Puccini—it made him feel ... *contento*, he said. So were they his hobbies? I asked. He shrugged his shoulders and could not answer. It was his work—it was productive, he said. He had no use for hobbies. He worked because he was alive.

A herb is never the boss

Pino grew many different herbs and as he worked he remembered what Maria, his mother, had told him. 'Lemon balm is for sympathy—a little bit is good but too much overpowers and can damage. Parsley seeds are slow to sprout because they must travel to the devil himself and back again before they can grow. Because of this, it is very unlucky to give parsley away but if you do, take a sprig of dill and wear it in your vest. It may itch but it will protect you from any bad luck. Rosemary also protects against evil and that is why we put it on coffins. It strengthens the brain and memory. The taste of rosemary honours all that has gone before. It is for remembrance.

'A good wife should have the virtues of marjoram, sage and tarragon. Marjoram is strong and courteous, and combines well with most things if treated with respect. Sage is soothing and brings with it beauty. A warning though, in large quantities it is ruined. Tarragon means "little dragon", because passion needs a little fire to keep the sparks alight. A wife with tarragon is the most precious wife of all. But Pino, a herb must never be the boss of the dish. It is like an afterthought—mysterious, never obvious.'

Pino thought about these things as he dug and weeded. As smells wafted from the ground and his nose waved around following the fragrance, he dreamed about the dishes he could create. Wild duck seasoned with sage and rosemary, dill cucumber and lemon balm, pork livers and fennel, ribbons of beans with parsley and tarragon. He told Jack his ideas but Jack scoffed. 'Listen, Pin,' he said, 'I don't mind yer givin' me a hand and I don't mind showing yer a thing or two, but don't go getting any bloody big ideas about cooking anything. It's not yer place. Know what I mean?'

When Pino returned to work in his garden he felt sad and subdued by Jack's words. A lone bird flew across the sky and he watched it glide and dip its wings. He remembered eating such a bird once. His father stunned it with a smooth round pebble that arched as gracefully as the bird did now. His mother had run to the bird, her small hands cradling it as tenderly as she would her own baby. Her fingers delicately encircled its neck—in an instant it was dead. She blessed herself, murmured thanks to God, and smiled at Pino. 'Tonight we eat meat. A feast.' Pino watched while she plucked the feathers and slit the bird open. He was sent to pick parsley, rosemary and celery leaves.

As Old Giuseppino led the prayer of thanks, Pino recalled how lightly the bird had flown and the soft thud of its body hitting the earth. Pino closed his eyes as he chewed, sweet juice squirting from the flesh. It tasted as wonderful as his mother had promised. He wondered whether it was possible that the bird was lighter in taste than it had been in flight?

He itched to cook like that, if only Jack would let him try.

The summer fruits at the orchard were nearing the end of their season. There was a big dance organised for Saturday night. The whole town was going to be there and Jack convinced Pino to go with him. 'Yer might see yer little girlfriend, introduce her to yer mate Jack,' he leered, for Pino had kept up the pretence of meeting someone while he secretly tended his garden. At the dance, Jack drank two bottles of whiskey and entertained everyone by playing the piano with his feet. Pino helped him home as the morning birds were starting their song. 'Pin, yer a bloody good mate—for a wog. Know what I mean?'

'Yeah, Jack, sure mate. Now get some sleep.'

'Pin, mate, the shit's really gunna hit the fan today. The boss is bringin' his missus for lunch. Let me get an hour of shut-eye and then givus a call.'

Pino began the breakfast preparations and called Jack a little later. 'Jack, mate,' but Jack lay perfectly still. His mouth was wide open and his tongue hung over his bottom lip. Pino wondered if he was dead and shook him gently, when Jack let out a snort that resonated through the cabin. 'Bloody hell,' Pino said, 'you scare the shit from me.' He shook Jack again but Jack slept on. Pino could see there would be no waking him in the next hour in time for breakfast. He would cook breakfast himself. It was just eggs and bacon fried in lard, and burnt toast. He had watched Jack do it hundreds of times, he knew he could do it too.

After breakfast he went back to Jack's cabin and still the big man slept on. Pino moaned. The boss was bringing his wife to the dining hall for lunch. It was a special occasion. Jack had planned roast beef, mashed potatoes, peas and carrots, followed by steamed pudding. Pino had an idea and wondered if he dared do it. Then he remembered his father and where he came from. He was a Portelli, one of the best. It was decided.

He would cook a meal so wonderful that all who tasted it would taste his home, smell his home, have a hunger for his home the way he did. He began chopping, peeling, dicing. He sprinted to his garden and grabbed handfuls of rosemary, parsley and garlic. He sliced and simmered, seasoned and sauteed. He rubbed the roast beef with garlic and cooked it slowly in a pot with sprigs of rosemary, diced celery and Jack's sherry. He sauteed the vegetables lightly so they were still firm, crisp on the outside but just softened inside. When the men lined up with their plates, some sniffed suspiciously. Pino watched anxiously as the boss and his wife ate. He noticed the smiles, the smacking of lips, the bread being used to mop up the juice. The men were quiet. Some even came back for seconds.

The boss went over to Pino at the end of the meal. 'Marvellous, Pin, bloody marvellous. Where has Jack been hiding you?' Pino blushed with pride—until he saw Jack, thunderous, in the corner. When everyone had left the dining hall, Jack stormed over to Pino. 'What the hell were yer thinkin', Pin? Yer poisoning these poor bastards!'

'Jack, just for once I wanted to cook a meal like my mamma.'

'Forget yer mamma, yer in Australia now, Pin. Yer eat Australian, see?'

'But the boss, he like it ...'

'The boss don't know shit. This is my kitchen, I'm the boss, see?'

And so Pino went back to peeling potatoes and scraping carrots. Often at meal times he caught the men looking over at him, but then Jack would boom out, 'Seconds anyone?' and the men would put their heads down and keep eating.

⌇

The Portellis are not my relatives but I call Pino 'Zio'—Uncle—
and his wife Valda 'Zia'. They are dear to me in a way my own
family will never be. Angelina says all Italians are related. 'They're
inbred,' she whispers. 'You ever been to the cemetery with my
ma? Now that's an experience. She used to drag me around the
cemetery carrying buckets of flowers and we'd have to stop and
cry at every frigging tomb. That really shows you everyone is
someone else's cousin, or sister, or sister's husband, or cousin's
sister's husband, or *someone*. Italians have the biggest families in the
world. No wonder Ma has been wearing black for a hundred
years—everyone who ever died is related to her. All those
Sundays I wasted walking around the cemetery. I tell you, you
don't know how lucky you are.'

How lucky I am ... I think over those words ... *how lucky I am*.
They are fat words full of despair, full of warning, hidden threats,
bonds, debts I can never repay.

They sound like a curse to me.

I know about curses. They are about silences between people,
lack of motion.

They are about blood.

Always.

Where there are curses there is always blood.

The blood in me is the curser and the cursed, mixed, facing
each other.

The curser and the cursed, together, in one circular path.

The curser is inflicted as much as the cursed.

The curser is eaten away, leaving only bitterness.

Residue.

The taste of green lemons.

To remember home—Pigeon in a pan

Chop a piece of salt-cured pork belly, 2 garlic cloves, 1 onion, 1 carrot, 1 celery stalk with leaves, a handful of parsley and rosemary. Mix in a pot and drizzle some olive oil over it. Place the pigeon on top and add salt and pepper. Pour one glass of red wine and sip to halfway while the pot cooks on a hot stove. As the pigeon browns, pour the rest of your wine over the top and turn the meat. Cover with a lid and let it simmer while you pour another glass of wine, sip half and pour the other half over the pigeon. Never drink more wine than you add to the pot, remembering excess of anything in life is no good for you.

PP

Pino pays his boys tuppence for every pigeon they kill. They make slingshots from rubber bands and bend coat-hangers, and find stones that fit the sling ...

The first time she has pigeon in a pan, Judy throws up and cannot eat for two days. The tiny bones on the plate upset her and she refuses ever to taste pigeon again, despite Pino begging her to try a mouthful. 'He is a barbarian,' she tells my father ...

Anthony loves pigeon in a pan. He licks the bones clean and then licks his fingers one by one ...

Graziella hunts through garbage tins at night and collects tiny bones to put in glass jars ...

Valda eats the pigeon, bones and all, saying it is a sin to waste food ...

2 Homemade pasta for patience

Appetiser	*My little chilli, let me be your bread*
Entree	*Good shoes make a good man*
Main course	*Dishonour and love*
	Extra-virgin olive oil
Dessert	*Love takes you home*

Zio Pino and Zia Valda do not speak to each other. They have been married for over thirty years and have not spoken for at least half that time, but there is no silence between them. This is difficult to explain to outsiders, who assume they must have an unhappy relationship, but I have never seen two people more passionate about each other than Zio and Zia.

Valda is Pino's chilli—
and Pino is Valda's salvation.

My little chilli, let me be your bread

When he came to Australia, Pino worked at an orchard for the first two years and then moved on to the city. He had heard from other workers that the city paid cooks well. Pino thought he could earn enough for a passage home in less than a year. On the day he left the orchard, Jack cooked a special treat: steak and kidney pie with mashed potatoes and mint peas. 'You Eyeties are the best bloody workers we got. I'll miss you, Pin, and remember, if you keep cookin' ...'

'Yeah, I know, mate, a bit of salt and a spoonful of dripping.' Pino looked up at Jack, 'Jack, you bin family to me. I ... I ...' He paused and drew a breath, searching for the words that would express how he felt about this man. This red giant with the gruff voice who had let Pino into his kitchen and been so willing to share his country. Even though Pino was an Eyetie, Jack had never questioned his right to be in Australia, to claim it for his own. Pino threw his arms around Jack. '*Ciao*, Jack, you bloody good mate.'

'Hey, mate.' Jack quickly disentangled himself from Pino's arms. 'Don't go turning poofter on me now.'

Pino liked the city. There were large markets and many Italians worked there. They called each other by name and haggled about prices, each arguing in their own dialect. If they found someone who came from their region they cried and hugged their new-found *paesano*. The market was stocked with such a huge range of fresh fruits and vegetables that it made Pino realise how rich the country was. Everything grew in the lucky country. After Jack's greasy ash-flavoured food, Pino's tastebuds were revived with enthusiasm. He found a guesthouse that was advertising for a kitchen hand and rented one of the rooms there. His job was peeling vegetables, getting the plates ready, and washing up. After two months of this the boss called him in one day and asked, 'Pino, how would you like to help with the cooking?'

'The cooking?' Pino clasped his hands and cried, 'Mr George, I bloody dream to do this. It's what my heart says my hands should do. To chop, and fry, and how you say? Season? So the flavour is just so! And the aroma, *beh!* It makes my nostrils sniff just to think of—'

'Hang on, Pino. I just want you to cook. You know, turn the steaks, mash the potatoes, dob some butter on the peas, get the idea?'

Pino visited the market extra early, while the stallholders were still setting up. He began to hunt out special ingredients: pine nuts, marjoram, young borage leaves, wild mushrooms. Mr George raised his eyebrows at some of the food but let him continue. Bill, the chief cook, was in awe of Pino's culinary prowess and encouraged him to do as he pleased. Bill told Mr George, 'I've never seen anyone do to food what Pino does, boss. He uses things that aren't even food and turns them into a bloody feast. It's because he's Catholic you know, it's one of them miracles. I remember at Sunday School they told us Jesus did it with a couple of loaves of bread but Pino does it every bloody day.'

One day at the market, Pino couldn't believe what he saw. Bucketfuls of shiny *ostriche,* calamari and mussels. The fisherman lifted the bucket and scooped some out. 'Mate, this is real good bait, thruppence for a dozen opened shells or tuppence for a dozen unopened.' Pino bought two dozen and could hardly wait to get back to the kitchen. When Mr George saw what he was doing he shook his head. 'You've gone too far this time, Pino, I won't allow you to poison my guests.' But Bill had faith. 'Let him go, boss. If he says he can feed us on fish bait let him try. Besides,' he added slyly, 'think of what a cheap meal this will be.'

Pino lightly sauteed the oysters and calamari and mussels in butter, added a morsel of garlic and a sprinkling of black pepper. He poured this sauce over steaming pasta and presented the plate to Mr George with a flourish, '*Spaghetti alla marinara*, spaghetti from the sea.' Mr George looked dubious. He'd caught beaut Tommy Ruffs with the bait in front of him. He called Bill. 'Here, you try it first.' Bill took a knife and fork and cut some of the spaghetti. He then scooped the pasta and some oysters into his mouth and winked at Pino. 'Smells great, mate.' They all watched as he chewed and swallowed and cut some more. 'Well?' Mr George asked, but Bill didn't say a word, just kept on eating. Finally, Mr George grabbed the spoon and put it into his mouth. 'Mmm,' he said, 'not bad. Not bad at all. It's sort of salty, buttery, with a fishy flavour ... It's bloody beautiful.' He laughed. 'Pino, you are a miracle worker.'

Pino was given a free rein in the kitchen. In his spare time he still liked to wander around the market. For him, a trip to the market was like a stroll through heaven. He met Valda at the market. She worked at the stall that sold the tiniest, hottest chillies. He later said he should have recognised that as an omen but at the time he was like a tastebud seduced by a *zabaglione*— dizzy with lightness.

Her black hair was as glossy as eggplant and he could just see the hair on her upper lip, like the fuzz of a tomato leaf. She was tiny—her head would just be level with his chest. He watched from behind the zucchinis as she called out non-stop in a nasal drawl. The other stallholders had complained about Valda's throaty calls. She said they were jealous of her because she attracted more customers. Pino was enraptured by the thick chocolate spill of her voice. 'Come an' get ba-naaah-na, aaah-ple, man-daaah-rine, to-maaah-to, po-taaah-to, caaah-rot ...' On and on she called, pacing across the front of the stall. It was then that he noticed her feet. As delicious as puffs of *montebianco* that took hours to whip until the egg whites were stiff peaks and the chestnut purée was as fluffy as a kitten. '*Montebianco*,' he mouthed adoringly as he watched. Her shoes were cheap-looking brown pumps, scuffed on the end, and he imagined her toes would be red and raw as squealing piglets. At night she would sit on the end of her bed and rub her tired feet.

He knew in that moment that this was a woman worth loving.

A hairy goddess with a voice and feet to match. He had to speak to her.

He pointed to the tomatoes. '*Scusi*,' his voice cracked. He cleared his throat and tried again, 'Are these fresh?' Valda had noticed him watching her and was glad he had finally come over to speak. She liked his face—she thought he looked like Saint Francis without the animals. 'All our food is fresh.' She flicked back her hair and exposed an ear, hairy down to the lobe. Pino felt weak in the knees and fought for some self-control. 'Not the cucumber,' he said.

'What do you mean?' snapped Valda.

'I bought some cucumber yesterday and it was all soggy. I had to throw it away.'

'Hah, you didn't buy it here.' Valda crossed her arms and looked up at him.

'*Si*, I bought it here ...'

'No, I didn't serve you,' she waved her finger at him.

'*Ma, si*,' he nodded and emphasised, 'a rotten cucumber.'

Valda puffed up her chest, her breasts were like new season pears and he resisted the urge to squeeze and test their freshness. She was delicious. He asked her out. 'Aaah, so, you make a joke with Valda just to ask her out, well I won't go with you. Anyway,' she pursed her lips, 'I am engaged to a fine man in Italy and we will be married when he comes to Australia.'

'I didn't ask you to marry me, just to come to a dance, at the church,' he held out his hands helplessly and smiled his most charming smile. He knew the power of that smile, having tested it many times back home.

'Aaah, but you will and then I will break your heart!' she said, and she turned her back on him and began unpacking the carrots.

Zio Pino tells me Zia Valda is as fiery as the chilli she once sold. 'Chilli is good,' he says. 'But on its own it burns itself out. The best chillies need to be eaten with a little bread to absorb the fire and give strength to the taste. When I first met Valda, I thought to myself, "My little chilli, let me be your bread."'

I look at my shoes lined up by the case. Brown suede walking boots, name brand runners, a nondescript pair of navy blue court shoes that match everything, black patent sling backs, and the leopard-skin stilettos. The stilettos feel as soft as a kitten and the leather smell is still as strong as when Zio Pino first gave them to me. I stick my nose in them and sniff greedily like a child guzzling a soft drink. They were handmade in Florence by a cobbler whose father learnt his craft from Zio's grandfather. They seem outrageously unnecessary. Yet, if it came to a choice between underwear or my skin stilettos I know which I'd choose. There is *necessary* unnecessary and *unnecessary* unnecessary. The secret is deciding which is which. When I wear the stilettos the leather clings like water to my feet and my feet look like they belong to someone else. Someone who knows who they are and where they are going. After I have worn them my legs ache, but some things in life are worth suffering for ...

'Only women suffer,' the *strega* said to me. 'That is why they bear the children. A man knows nothing about pain, real pain.' When she said this she looked into my eyes and I knew she could see inside me. I felt scared but sorry too. Sorry for her that she seemed to know so much about pain. I even prayed for her on Sundays but she didn't want my prayers—she wanted my soul.

Homemade pasta for patience

'Patience,' my mother Maria would say, 'is not about time, or how quickly or slowly you do something. It is about attention. To be patient is to be attentive, to appreciate the fine details.'

Cut a reed from the banks of a river. It must be long and smooth, wash it and make sure you dry it thoroughly.

Mix 3 cups of durum wheat flour with 2 eggs, maybe three if the eggs are not so big. Mix to a dough that is as soft as a woman but as strong as a mother's love. Roll it very thin and cut strips as wide as a finger. Roll the pasta strip around the reed, pinching the sides together. Carefully, with patience, slide the pasta tube off the reed and hang it away from the draught to dry.

PP

Pino cuts and rolls each strip—strand by strand. He picks up a piece of the soft golden dough so deftly that he barely makes an indentation in it. He rolls it over a reed and uses his thumb to pinch the sides together. His actions are painstakingly slow and he sings a sad love song, '*E Lucevan le Stelle*', drawing out each word as long as he can. He slides the fragile tube off the reed and hangs it over the chair to dry as he sings, '*E non ho amato mai tanto la vita!*' ...

Valda waits for God. She prays on her knees and rolls the beads of her rosary rhythmically. Usually, she likes to do things fast, get on with the job, but when she prays, she is content to wait ...

Graziella cries thirteen tears into the tiny glass bottle. She will save these for thirteen days before she uses them in her mixtures ...

Judy can never wait. She wants things done yesterday and is an impatient driver. She beeps her horn a lot when she drives and gets stressed easily. She tried relaxation classes but couldn't bear sitting around not doing anything when the class was relaxing ...

I spend my whole life waiting. It is action that scares me ...

Good shoes make a good man

Pino could think of nothing but Valda after he spoke to her at the market. He stopped eating. Even the most tantalising aromas did not arouse him. Love had blocked his nose.

For the next month he was at the market by five a.m. every morning. He helped Valda's boss, Guido Sabato, unload his truck. Guido was twenty years older than Pino and had been disfigured by a serious motorcycle accident. Guido accepted Pino's help but spoke very little, just grunted, like a carnivorous animal. Pino didn't speak to Valda during this time. He recalled the times back home when he helped Maria to cook. He often lifted the lid of the pan impatiently, to see if the water had boiled. Maria chastised him as she sprinkled the salt over the salad. 'Pino,' she said, 'the salt of patience seasons everything that is tasty.'

So he was patient. After a month of helping at the market, Guido finally invited Pino to his house for a meal. It was what Pino had been waiting for. Valda lived with Guido and his wife, Graziella, and she would be at the lunch. Pino planned to impress her with his good looks and charm. He knew she would be begging him to ask her out by the end of the day. He could hardly wait.

He took out his finest clothes—which were not so fine any more—but his shoes were good, handmade in Florence. They were worth a month's salary and it was only when he had asked himself, *What would Papà do?* that he had decided to buy them. He knew his father the cobbler would be pleased. Old Giuseppino called shoes *casine*—little houses. He said they housed the feet and the feet were sacred to our view of the world. 'Our feet connect us to the earth, while our head aspires to the heavens. It is an ill-tempered man who wears badly fitted shoes, for the connection to the earth is broken and pained, and he does not stand solidly. The toes should be spread flat, the arch slightly lifted, as in all aspects of life, there should be balance. The weight of the body balances across the ball of the feet and the heels. Good shoes make a good man.'

Pino shined his shoes until they were as slick as still water, he cleaned his teeth three times, twice with charcoal to whiten them and once with brandy to keep them strong. He smoothed his hair down, set his hat at a jaunty angle and looked in the mirror. He was beautiful, how could Valda resist him?

Guido's house was the largest in the street, set on a huge block with a winding driveway that circled the front. Two pink concrete flamingos stood on either side of the front verandah and a miniature concrete waterfall was in the middle of the lawn. Wrought iron balustrades painted bright blue adorned the entrance. But what most surprised Pino was the small child's bicycle next to the front door. Guido had never mentioned having children.

Pino felt the breath catch in his throat as the tallest woman he had ever seen opened the door and stood before him. She was as tall as Jack, bigger maybe, with startling blue eyes and pale straw-coloured hair that was piled on her head, making her appear even taller. Her aquiline nose hung over a mouth that looked like she had sipped something sour.

He could not speak.

'Are you Pino?' she asked in a slow rounded voice, eyeing him from head to toe. He was glad of his shoes and felt a little bolder—he even put a foot forward onto the step and smiled. The woman did not smile back. 'I am Graziella. Guido's wife.' She pushed the door open and it squashed Pino's toes. He yelped and jumped back. He looked down and saw that the steel-framed door had scratched across his leather shoe. He looked from the shoe to Graziella, to the shoe again, and then held out the two bunches of white chrysanthemums he had brought. 'Flowers,' Graziella annunciated, 'how civil.' She took both bunches and shoved them at Valda who was standing behind her in the hallway. 'Put these in water,' she said.

Pino was stunned. Graziella sounded like an Italian name but the woman before him was surely not Italian. He could just detect a trace of an accent as she spoke. It was not so much in the way the words were pronounced but in the overall sound. It was as if the music of the language was off-key. He followed her into a large room with an ornate ceiling rose in the centre and a grandfather clock ticking in the corner. Guido was already seated at the table, a glass of red wine in front of him. He grunted at Pino.

Graziella sat. 'You are very honoured, Pino. My husband doesn't usually invite guests. Especially for meals,' she snarled. Pino could only wonder what she meant by this. Valda brought out sherries for Pino and Graziella, and a bowl of salted peanuts. Pino waited for Valda to sit with them but each time she did Graziella sent her back to the kitchen for something else. Valda obeyed uncomplainingly but the way she flicked back her hair and pushed out her chin told Pino she was not born to serve. He recognised that she had too much tarragon in her. When she was in the kitchen he heard her banging pots and muttering curses in Italian but when she came out she smiled sweetly at Graziella and coyly at Pino. As she placed the mashed potatoes and sausages in front of him he caught a whiff of her garlic breath. He breathed it in and sighed. He thought it was as fragrant as the sweetest perfume.

Graziella was an indifferent hostess. She poked at her food and nibbled small mouthfuls with distaste. Guido hardly spoke, just sat, hunched over his plate shovelling mouthful after mouthful in and never pausing for a breath. He ate as if at any moment his meal was going to be snatched away from him. Pino was surprised by the meal, which reminded him of his cooking days with Jack. Nothing from the large range of herbs and vegetables that Guido sold was included. He suspected that it was Graziella's doing. The only thing she seemed passionate about was that he refrain from speaking Italian in her house. She even pronounced it the way the Australians did—Eyetallion. 'We live in Australia now, we are Australians. Only the ignorant continue to pay homage to a back- ward land so far away.' At this point she glared at Valda who stared back. She went on saying, 'This is the better country, it is the better language. Don't you agree?' He didn't. Nor did he see that it came down to one being better than the other. But as he looked into those pale eyes he didn't dare utter a sound.

Graziella farted three times during lunch. The first time Pino looked down at his plate, shocked. He felt a little kinder towards her, thinking the poor woman must be so embarrassed. The second time he nearly laughed and had to disguise it as a cough— no one else seemed aware that anything unusual had happened. The third time he wasn't sure he heard anything but there was no mistaking Graziella's shift in her seat, leaning on her left side and raising her right buttock slightly so she could push the fart out. This was the one that smelt the worst. Pino was bewildered as the others sat, impassively eating. He was just wondering whether he had imagined it all when Graziella burped, a gaseous belch that hit him square in the face. There could be no mistaking it. She stared at him with such dislike that Pino felt paralysed and could not move his eyes from her face. She spat the words out, 'I have a digestive disorder.' Pino nodded. He felt he should say something but every time he tried he forgot the English words and the Italian ones were out before he realised it. The harder he tried the worse he was, so he sat, mute, staring into his dessert, a lumpy pudding he could barely swallow.

He was just wondering how he could possibly remember the words for 'thank you' and 'goodbye' when a tall, thin child came into the dining room.

Anthony had light curly hair and huge brown eyes, with a faint crease from frowning already set between his eyebrows. He stood next to Graziella, a tall boy with thin arms and rounded shoulders. Graziella said, 'This is Mr Portelli. Pino, my son Anthony.'

'Hello, sir,' Anthony lisped.

Pino smiled and held out his hand, 'Antonio, *piacere*!' he said.

'Anthony.' Graziella's voice cut as sharp as a blade, 'His name is Anthony. Stand straight now, Anthony, don't slouch.'

Later, Anthony took Pino to the back garden to see his work bench. In the tool shed he had broken clocks, watches, an iron and even a broken box brownie camera. 'I like fixing things,' he told Pino.

'How old are you?'

'Seven years old, sir.'

'Oh, please, call me Pino, you know, that's my name,' Pino shrugged and smiled.

'Don't you ever smile?' he teased.

'Not often, sir,' was the solemn reply.

Pino didn't stay for coffee and Valda was allowed to walk him to the front gate. As soon as they were away from the house Pino exploded, 'Oh, my God, are they always like that? Is that woman a witch?'

Valda whispered, 'Graziella cannot control the noises her body makes and we never comment on them. You poor boy, I cheer you up. I go with you to the dance next month but you must ask Graziella's permission and don't let her know I already say yes.' She skipped inside, laughing at him. He shook his head. He had planned to impress Valda with his sophistication and charm; instead she was going out with him because she felt sorry for him.

Dishonour and love

They were married in the spring. Valda made her own wedding gown as well as Graziella's matron-of-honour dress. She sent the invitations, booked the church and decorated the hall. Graziella never once offered to help and Valda was too proud to ask. She wrote to her parents and told them she was to be married, disregarding her betrothal to Claudio Moroni. They answered her letter with a telegram of three words, 'Come Home Immediately.' Valda read the telegram over and over. She knew the dishonour she would bring to her family by breaking her engagement. When Valda was five, her older sister had run off with a German toolmaker and brought disgrace to her family. The responsibility to make amends for her sister had fallen on Valda's shoulders and she had dutifully taken it on. But she had been away from home for six years now and never once had Claudio answered the weekly letters she wrote to him. She barely remembered what he looked like. Besides, she had her suspicions about his fidelity. Finally, she screwed the telegram up and threw it in the bin. Pino was her family now, that was all that mattered.

❧

When I was ill and could not eat, Zia Valda sat by my bed feeding me her love story to make me strong.

Extra-virgin olive oil

Valda remembers her wedding night as clearly as if it were yesterday. Pino gently leading her out of the bathroom where she had been hiding from him. They had never been alone in the time they had courted. She knew little of the ways of love and had grown used to Graziella and Guido shrieking and grunting in the night. Pino caressed her hair, and although she trembled at his touch he did it so calmly that she relaxed, and, in spite of her fear, enjoyed the feel of his small hand stroking her head.

For the first three nights of their marriage she slept in his arms as he stroked her hair. On the fourth—and she took this as an omen that they would have four children—he sniffed as his hand unleashed the scent of her hair. She had washed it that day in an infusion of rosemary, lavender and tarragon, mixed with a drop of extra-virgin olive oil. He sniffed handfuls of her glossy hair and she felt strangely excited by this closeness. He moved his nose along her head, pressing it to her scalp, sniffing. He sniffed the nape of her neck and she felt tingles ring through her as sharp and clear as the communion bell at mass. When he hesitated at her neck it was she who turned to him and, with both hands, reached for his nose and stroked it gently, kissing it on the tip. He moved his nose all over her; sniffing and licking her underarms, between her breasts, along her legs, her feet—where he sniffed the cheesy odour between each toe.

He moved on top of her and it was only then that she became aware that the urgency she felt inside, the ache, was coming from her woman's part. He seemed to know this before she did.

Zia Valda told me the story of her love without blushing. Her eyes half-closed, her fat body swaying gently in the chair, a strong woman unafraid of her desires. She is beautiful.

Love takes you home

Valda thought of God that night, as Pino moved inside her. She prayed it was not a sin—because it felt so good—but deliriously knew it *had* to be a sin—because it felt so good.

'Sweet Jesus,'
>   she moaned
'Glory be to the Father,'
>   as she moved
'and the Son,'
>   she couldn't stop
'And the Holy Spirit,'
>   her woman's thing was swallowing him.
And as she called,
'Amen, Amen, Amen!'

She knew it had been a sin because some part within had awoken and melted in her.

Each day Pino delighted in feeding Valda tastes she had never had before. She came from a poor family and was familiar with the bite of hunger. When she came to Australia with Graziella there was plenty of food but the taste was dull. With Pino there were flavours she had never dreamed of, and her appetite was endless. She ate everything he offered; he told her he loved to watch her eat. He was a man who constantly left her wondering, saw beauty in things she didn't notice, smelt aromas she couldn't smell. His heart soared to invisible places. He had a way about him. When he cooked he sang operas and threw in ingredients, never measuring but always knowing how much was exactly right. He did every-thing by feel, passionately, with his whole spirit. When he spoke, men listened and women watched. People remembered him, his fine face, his stylish dress. She was proud to be seen with him.

That summer they made *salsa* from cases of overripe tomatoes. He slipped a sprig of basil into each bottle and stored them under the bed and in the wardrobe of their tiny two-roomed flat. Valda worked from dawn to midday at the market and Pino worked all night at the guesthouse. But in the early afternoon they came together to share their dreams. He cooked a light *brodo* with a sprinkling of tarragon and told her stories of his home; seasoning the memories with his father's wise voice and the gentle ways of his mother. Memories folded with music, songs, the smell of his people; memories whipped to peaks of gaiety; memories that made his heart ache.

They decided to save and go back to his village.

'If it makes you smile, I smile too,' Valda told him. But in her heart, she did not want to go. She belonged here, in this new country. She felt young in a way she had not felt before. And for all the times Pino talked of 'back home' she never saw him being anywhere other than right where he was. But she also knew he was a man. He needed to have somewhere outside himself, a tan-gible that he could hang onto and say, 'Here, this is where I belong. This is who I am.' Women were different. They carried their sense of self with them no matter where they were. She knew she could follow him anywhere and still be happy. It was her gift to him.

Later, when she decided to stop talking to him, that had also been a gift. Her way of saving face for herself and him. She understood the importance of this, for who can live without a face?

3 Sugo cooked by sunshine

Appetiser   *Carlo quello con la faccia bella*

Entree   *Equilibrio––Balance*

Main course   *Similar but not the same*

Dessert   *I love you now and forever*

I close Zio Pino's case and swing the make-up bag over my shoulder. I know Judy will be disappointed I haven't used the other cases but the make-up bag should be of some consolation to her. I grab my ventolin and a burst of gas hits my throat. I don't ever remember seeing her without make-up. She says it gives her strength to look at the world. 'I'll just put on a face,' she says. And you know, she really does believe it is that easy. She tells me I have to 'face up to things, accept responsibility'. I try but it is not so easy. I talked to Zio about it once and he told me the story of Carlo, the beautiful faced one.

Carlo quello con la faccia bella

'My father, Old Giuseppino, told me about a boy he grew up with, Carlo was his name. Carlo was a handsome boy. He had golden skin and black curly hair, his eyes were like the sky at midnight and his teeth were like the stars. When he went to market, older women were charmed by his good looks and gave him extra vegetables. When he went to help in the fields the men were struck with nostalgia by his youthful manliness. His rippling muscles, his strength and vitality, it reminded them of how they once were, so they let him sleep under the elm tree and stay fresh and unsoiled by the sweat of hard work. One day when the soldiers came to town they took Carlo and fed him and gave him a handsome uniform cut from fine cloth with many shiny buttons.

'Carlo saw his reflection and was so dazzled by the dashing figure he had become that he forgot to listen to what the soldiers were saying. He believed anyone who looked so fine must be good. So Carlo went away with the soldiers. Many years later the soldiers returned with a General who was noted for wearing a wide-brimmed hat that shadowed his face. It was rumoured that the General had no face, that it had been blown away in a battle. But when the soldiers came and stole Old Giuseppino's cobbler's last and threw it into the Pit of the Abyss, the General stayed back and spoke to the cobbler. He took off his hat and Old Giuseppino saw that the tired old General was Carlo, his boyhood friend. Carlo embraced Old Giuseppino and begged his forgiveness for what his soldiers had done. "I did it to save your life, old friend," Carlo said. "There is no place among the conquered for a man with face. I had to destroy your cobbler's last for what it represented. It is nothing really, you and I both know you are the same person without it but if I did not do it you would be dead. Let them think they have beaten you but keep your face." To which my father asked, "And you Carlo, where is your face?" Carlo shook his head, "That is why I wear my hat, old friend. I no longer have a face. It is a terrible thing for a man to live without a face. All that you see is not all that there is. This I have learned." To which my father invited Carlo to share our meal. The neighbours threw

stones at our window for dining with the General and my father
never told them who he really was. My mother cooked *baccalà* for
us that night. It was the next day that my father called me aside
and told me I must leave. And so I left.'

Pino looked at me and lifted my chin with his index finger.
'Always keep your face, little one,' he said.

I take a taxi to the airport. Judy wanted to drive me but I insisted
I would meet her there. 'I live on the other side of town. It's silly
for you to drive all the way here and then have to go back again,'
I said.

'You're right,' she agreed. 'Your father hasn't been well and
shouldn't drive too far, we would go through double the amount
of petrol to get there.'

I hang up the telephone and feel disappointed. If Zia and Zio
were my parents they would have driven me no matter how far
it was. That is what families do—they go out of their way for each
other without thinking twice about it. But Judy does think twice.
She weighs up every word and measures it and tries it out and
considers all the other possibilities.

My taxi driver is Lebanese. He has two jobs and is saving to
bring his wife and children out from Lebanon. He has not seen
them for two years. He asks me where I am going. 'Italy,' I reply.

'Aaah,' he shakes his head knowingly. 'The Italians, they are
very good workers.'

Equilibrio—Balance

Italians know how to work because they *mantengono un senso di equilibrio*, they keep their balance. Pino said, 'To work hard we must play hard. Too much one way is no good. When an Italian works he works for himself, his family and for God. He has *equilibrio*.'

That was how Pino survived the four years he held two full-time jobs. He worked at the guesthouse from late afternoon until nearly midnight. He had five hours to rest before he was at work again, labouring on a building site, wheeling barrowfuls of bricks and mortar for the bricklayers. The bricklayers were mainly Italians, men with ruddy faces and big rough hands. Pino could tell which village they were from by their dialect and they each argued the virtues of their region. He made many friends: Vincenzo Dimasi, Dominic Cirrillo, Pasquale Cavallaro. On days when Pino felt the sun burn into his shoulders, and heat his head until he wished he could rip his hair out, Vincenzo showed him how to make a hat from his handkerchief. Pino dipped the knotted cloth into a bucketful of water and then spread it over his head. The relief was immediate—although always short lived, for the cloth dried stiff and hard very quickly.

As he struggled with the wheelbarrow, Pino kept his mind off the heat and the ache in his arms and back by thinking of new dishes to cook. What would happen, he wondered, if he added anjelica to chicken? What other herb could he use on beef? How would a pinch of chilli taste added to the mashed potatoes—would it add a little zest to the flavour? If he wasn't cooking in his mind he kept alert by remembering the operas his mother Maria sang along to, for Maria always played music as she cooked. Her most prized possession, apart from her large copper cooking pot, was a gramophone player Old Giuseppino had given her for her twenty-fifth birthday. She often told Pino how surprised she had been that day when Old Giuseppino lead her into the *salotto*, his hands over her eyes—even before they were there she heard the sounds she had heard as a child—the Great Voices.

Maria's mother Lucia had been a serving girl in the great Puccini's household. Often during the day, as Lucia baked and little Maria helped her, Signor Puccini would come into the kitchen and sit by the warm stove. He ate nothing for breakfast, only drank scalding cups of black coffee, but for lunch he relished a big meal. He was generous with his money, always giving Lucia more than she asked for when she went shopping. He demanded that the house always have plenty of food. While he had been studying at the Conservatory he had been forced to eat frugally, because he was so poor. Minestrone, gorgonzola cheese and black bread had been his daily diet.

He loved Lucia's apple tart and asked her to make it every week. While she peeled the apples he would sit by the stove balancing little Maria on his knee and ask Lucia to sing for him. She always refused. But then he begged and said, 'Maria, tell your mamma I can't live another moment without hearing her golden song. She must sing. She has the voice of a bird, the sweetest bird that ever sang.' And Maria giggled as she, too, begged her mamma until Lucia blushed and smiled and said yes, she would sing—but only one song. Then Lucia sang in her golden voice and Maria watched as Signor Puccini let his head gently sway from side to side with a look of rapture on his face. When Lucia finished singing, Signor Puccini kissed her hand and said, '*Grazie, mia Mimi.*' He always called Lucia Mimi although Maria did not know why.

Maria wished Signor Puccini was her father. When she went for rides in his automobile and sat up the front with him, as the machine rattled and wheezed its way along, she pretended he was. She did not know her father—he had been a soldier and died before she was born. He had been Signor Puccini's friend. But while Maria loved Signor Puccini, she avoided his wife Signora Elvira as much as possible.

Signora Elvira had a harsh shrill voice and always complained about Lucia's cooking. The milk for the *caffè latte* was not scalded enough, the *minestra* was not thick enough, the vegetables were soft, the meat was tough. She hit Lucia across the back with a switch from an elm tree and told her she was a foolish girl. She yelled at Signor Puccini but he never raised his voice in reply, just listened, and then wrote music and words that rose to dizzying heights and made singers open their voices to dance with the music. He told Maria the voice was the greatest instrument of all. 'We all have a single sound, a tone, that resonates inside and gives us voice,' he said in his own quiet voice. 'Our voice lets the world know who we are.' And then he would pat Maria sadly on the head and go back to the *salotto* where he sat by the piano writing music. Maria listened to the music, sad and tragic, yet happy and glorious, and knew it was about love. She thought love must be like being caught in a raging fire; trapped, all consumed, the only release—death.

At night, Lucia made hot lemon tea with honey, brandy and a pinch of black pepper. It was Maria's job to serve this to Signor Puccini in the *salotto*. He suffered from chronic sore throat and swore that Lucia's tea was the only beverage that relieved his condition. Often he worked all through the night and called for pots of tea at all hours. Then Lucia would patiently rise from her bed and serve him herself.

Maria lived with the Puccinis until she was eight. That was the year Signor Puccini wrote *La Bohème* and became a great success. There were many parties at the house and Lucia and Maria were always busy. One night, Signor Puccini came into the kitchen and took Lucia by the hand. 'Come,' he begged. 'Sing for them all so they know how it is meant to sound.' He took her into the *salotto* and played the music from his newest opera. Lucia sang '*Mi Chiamo Mimi*' in her clear pure voice and Puccini's friends all clapped and cheered when she finished. Maria felt so proud of her mother. That night, she dreamed her mother was in the opera, dressed in the finery Maria had seen the singers wear, and with her face powdered and painted.

The next morning when Maria woke, her mother was gone. Signora Elvira called Maria into the *salotto* and told her she was being sent to the convent where the nuns would care for her. She said Lucia had gone and Maria was never to think of her again. Maria did not believe her mother would abandon her but was too scared of Signora Elvira to question her. For the next eight years Maria lived with the nuns, sleeping in a small room that had only a wooden cot and crucifix on the wall. Her days were kept busy with chores: scrubbing the stairs, the doors, working in the kitchen. She did not make friends with the other girls who were orphans. She told them about her mother. 'She will come back for me soon and I will leave this wretched place,' she said. At night she cried into her pillow wondering why her mother had left her. Every birthday a parcel arrived with no card and she told the girls it was from her mother. There were ribbons for her hair, English toffees and once, surprisingly, American cigarettes that she hid from the nuns and smoked outside the garden shed.

On her sixteenth birthday, a small parcel arrived. Inside were two tickets to the opening night of *Madame Butterfly*, Puccini's newest opera, and a pair of gold earrings in the shape of butter-flies. Each one had a single diamond in the centre. When the Mother Prioress saw them she said because it was Maria's birthday she could wear them to the opera but after that she could donate them to the convent.

It was a frightening night. Puccini had many enemies who were envious of his success and the crowd was hostile from the start. They threw cabbages and booed and hissed, some even barked like dogs. But Maria was captivated by Butterfly, and in the final scene, when Butterfly thrust the sword into her heart, Maria felt the pain grip her own heart as she realised for the first time that her mother was never coming back. Maria knew her mother was dead.

When she returned to the convent she waited until everyone was asleep and then sneaked out the kitchen door. It was raining and all she had on was a thin pinafore and her butterfly earrings but she ran and ran until she could run no more and she dropped with exhaustion in a barn and slept. For the next three days she walked in the rain, not eating, just drinking a little, not knowing where she was going but knowing she had to keep going. Old Giuseppino and his father found her collapsed on the roadside. They carried her to their wagon and took her home. She had a burning fever for many weeks and when she was well she did not speak. Old Giuseppino visited her every day and spoke to her. He did not seem to notice that she didn't answer his questions. He told her about his day, the shoes he had made, how the leather was the finest in all of Italy, how his father had let him use the mallet to mould the shoe into shape. When Maria did finally speak, after months of silence, Old Giuseppino was already in love with her. They were soon married and it was only after several years that she told him about her past, where she had lived, and her mother. That was when Old Giuseppino bought her the gramophone player and recordings of Puccini's operas. She listened to them all—except *Madame Butterfly*. She cooked to them, told her son Pino it enhanced the flavour—the sounds permeated the food and sweetened the taste. And although Pino had no facilities to play the opera as he cooked at the guesthouse, he sang and hummed along to the tunes in his head. He believed they not only sweetened the taste but sweetened life. That was why he sang as he wheeled the barrows through concrete dust and mud to the bricklayers.

His boss was an English man. Vincenzo called him 'the Pommy'. He was always complaining about the cost of the building materials and how the workers weren't what they used to be. The men listened to his complaints and nodded sympathetically and said they would try to work faster to finish the job. But when he was out of sight Vincenzo would call them to stop work and have a smoko. 'We are well ahead with this job. He wants it finished yesterday, eh, he can wait until tomorrow. All things can wait, it is the way of the world. Trust me.' Later, Vincenzo would go and see the boss, holding his hat in his hands, eyes cast downwards. He was so sorry, he would tell the boss, but the bricks had not arrived and they had not been able to start on the west wall as they had hoped. The boss would sigh and complain out loud. 'Why does this always happen? Every time we are ahead of schedule and look like finishing the job early something happens to hold us up.' Vincenzo assured him they would get the job done. He could convince the men to work twice as hard if they had some sort of incentive, 'Eh?' he winked and rubbed his fingers together. Pino watched this exchange, laughing to himself. Vincenzo, he was sure, was *mafioso*.

At lunch time the men would bring out thermoses of thick black coffee sweetened with four sugars and a dash of brandy. And they would swap their salami rolls for leftover lasagne wrapped in brown paper and woollen socks to keep it warm. Sometimes, someone's wife would come, carrying a small saucepan wrapped in a tea towel. She would stand back shyly as her husband ate and invited his workmates to share his food. They would wave their forks around as they talked and when they were finished, the empty saucepan would be handed back to the wife and each man would nod his head respectfully and thank the signora for the

meal. Often Pino would enquire what oil the signora had used.
What herb? Had she ever tried using borage instead of sage? And
the signora would blush, grateful for the attention of the charming
man whose khaki shorts had sharp creases starched into them and
whose work boots shone from their daily brushing.

One day, Valda came to the building site. The men stood
around as Pino introduced her, waiting for the saucepan of food
to materialise. But Valda had not brought food. She nodded
politely to all the men and then pulled Pino aside and whispered
in his ear. Pino gave a shriek and scooped Valda off the ground,
dancing around with her. 'Mamma mia,' he yelled, 'I'm going to
be a papà.' The men hugged Valda and kissed Pino on both
cheeks.

'You know, if it's a boy, Vincenzo is a fine name,' Vincenzo
told Valda.

'No, sorry,' Pino held up his hand and said, 'if it's a boy it's
going to be called Giuseppino after my father.'

'I think, myself, that it will be a girl,' Valda said.

The men laughed. Vincenzo said, 'With respect, Signora, the
first baby is always a boy.'

'I think, not this time,' Valda said sweetly.

With a baby on the way, Pino was more determined than ever
to take his family back to his village. He never felt tired, knowing
that each moment he was working meant money was being saved.
He cooked and wheeled barrows of bricks and puffed out his chest
as he sang, and dreamed of his son, little Giuseppino.

When the baby was born, Valda was worried that Pino would
be disappointed. But when he held his daughter for the first time,
saw her hairy ears and wrinkled face, sniffed her creamy skin, he
cried and thanked God, knowing he could never make a soufflé as
sweet, as soft. 'Angelina,' he called her. 'My little Angel.'

Angelina was a good baby who fed and slept with a quiet ease.

Valda went back to work at the market and Angelina spent the day sleeping behind the zucchini crates. When, at six months, she started teething, Valda cut strips of celery and artichoke for her to gnaw on. For Angelina, vegetables were her first play things and later in life if ever she felt unhappy or upset she ate vegetables for comfort. She told me she enjoyed meats and breads and pastas but for all her father's culinary genius there was nothing quite like a warm, freshly picked tomato or the funky reek of a mushroom.

Plans were made for the christening. Pino sent to Italy for a lace christening gown that cost £10 and he asked Vincenzo and his wife Carmella to be Angelina's godparents. Angelina had charmed Vincenzo from the moment he saw her by squeezing his big rough finger in her tiny hand. He had five sons yet he envied Pino his little angel. Pino hired the local church hall and invited everyone he knew: Graziella and Guido, workmates, customers from the guesthouse and the market, the people from the local milkbar, the paperboy and his family—there were three hundred guests in total. Pino supervised the catering. First, antipasto—provelone cheese, black olives, prosciutto, and pickled vegetables; then pasta—homemade ravioli with a Neapolitan sauce. Next—half a crayfish and king prawns. The main meal was in two parts—chicken and string beans followed by veal and potatoes.

Men ate and ate until they could see the bottom of their plates and women discreetly wrapped prawns and veal in paper serviettes and squashed them into their brown leather handbags—muttering all the while about what a shame it would be for the uneaten food to be thrown out. Graziella was the only one who seemed unimpressed by the food. She nibbled on a pickled carrot and refused everything else. She had not been well, she told Vincenzo when he tried to coax her into trying the ravioli. 'Eyetallion food does not agree with me,' she said.

'Bullshit! *Scusi*, Signora, but Italian food agrees with everyone, eh?' He laughed, looking around for support, but Graziella stood and towered over him.

'I will not stay here and be insulted by an ignorant peasant such as yourself,' she said.

She walked off as Vincenzo called out apologies, '*Scusi*, Signora, I make a joke ...' and when she did not respond he shrugged and made a rude gesture with his fist in the air.

Pasquale brought out his piano accordion. The men linked arms and danced as they sang and the women clapped. When the coffee and cream cakes were served, they drank and ate as they stood in groups and argued about the soccer, the best time to make wine, the virtues of their region. Vincenzo said the region he came from was well known for its virile men. 'You know, women always want my body. Even the *Australiane* women stare at me with lust.' He tapped his chest. 'It is because the male children from my region have a wet nurse until they are thirteen. The milk from the bosom makes them ...' he rocked his hips back and forward, '*robusti*.'

Graziella looked for Guido. Her stomach felt hard and full of gas and she wanted to leave. She found Guido asleep in the corner, drunk. She took the car keys from his pocket and looked for her son. Anthony was in the kitchen sitting next to the cradle watching Angelina sleep. She had slept through the whole party and nearly through the christening ceremony. It was only when Father Tolmino poured the water on her head that she had cried. Valda had blessed herself then, thankful, for it was bad luck for a baby not to cry at a christening—it meant the devil was still inside.

Graziella grabbed her son. 'Anthony, we are leaving.'

'But Valda said I could feed Angelina when she wakes.'

'We are leaving. Now.' They went out to the car without saying goodbye.

'Who's going to drive, Mum?' Anthony asked when he didn't see Guido.

'I am.' As Graziella revved the engine and crunched the gears, Anthony guessed why he had never seen his mother drive before.

At midnight, Pino called for everyone's attention—dessert was to be served, he announced. Thirty flaming Bombe Alaska were brought out. The crowd cheered at the spectacular display, which was unlike anything they had ever seen before. But the cheers soon turned to screams as the local fire brigade burst in with hoses and axes demanding to be led to the fire. Apparently they had been alerted that the church hall was filled with smoke. Pino assured them there was no fire and invited them to stay for dessert. When they left, they gave Guido a ride home.

By three a.m. Vincenzo and Carmella, Pasquale and Teresa, Dominic and Maria were the only guests remaining. Vincenzo brought out a bottle of *grappa* and the men drank and sang until they had no voices left. Angelina Portelli's christening lived long in their memories.

Similar but not the same

Three months later, Valda visited the building site again.

'Signora Valda,' Vincenzo called, picking Angelina up from her pram, 'how is my little Angel?'

'Very well, thank you,' Valda smiled. 'Pino, I have something to tell you.' She whispered something and Pino looked at her. 'Are you sure?' he asked. She nodded shyly. '*Madonna*,' he called, 'I'm going to be a papà again.'

'And this time,' Valda said, 'it will be a boy. Little Giuseppino.' But Pino shook his head. 'No. My father was right. A man should have his own name. He will be Giuseppe, similar but not the same.'

With the second pregnancy, Valda had to leave work at the market after only a month. Her legs were swollen and she could not stand for too long. As she lay in bed alone at night, waiting for Pino to return from work, she used his pillow to prop up her feet and relieve the dull ache. Pino often slept sniffing the cheesy pong of Valda's feet. It made him dream of *sugo* sprinkled with golden *parmigiano*.

Sugo cooked by sunshine

In cooking, the best cooked foods are those cooked simply, not over-fussy. Sharp and clean. The sunshine here is different to the sunshine back home. This is a sauce I only learnt to make here. Full of the Australian sun.

Pick 6 tomatoes 1 hour before the sun goes down so they are full of the warmth of the day. Split them and squeeze the juice in a bowl and chop the tomatoes. Heat some oil with a clove of garlic. Mix the tomatoes with the warm oil and sprinkle fresh basil over it.

Spoon this over steaming pasta.

Buonissimo!

PP

Pino sniffs the tomato. It has a warm earthy smell that speaks to him of the musty soil and hot Australian sun. 'I love the smell of fresh tomatoes—they hold their home in them.

'As much as I missed back home, I chose to stay here. You know why?' He slits the ripe red skin and gently squeezes. 'Love. Well, love and basil made me stay.' He takes the basil and chops it with a quick vibrating action. 'Did you know that basil is the symbol of love but it cannot grow unless it is abused and sworn at while the seed is sown? I have seen people plant basil and feed it and water it and shelter it from too much sun and instead of blooming it withers and dies. It takes a sharp tongue to grow good basil. I am the same. Your Zia Valda has a tongue sharper than the finest blade, eh,' he shrugs, 'that is love.' ...

Valda is mopping the floor with vinegar. Angelina walks in and slumps over the kitchen bench. 'Ma, I'm so depressed,' she says. Valda stops mopping and looks over at her.

'What's this mean de-press-ed?'

'I'm unhappy, heartbroken, *depressione, capisci?*'

'Mmmm.' She thinks for a moment and then asks, 'Show me your purse.'

'My purse, why?'

'Eh, do as you told.'

Angelina opens her purse. She has two twenty-dollar bills and a five. Valda takes the two twenties.

'Hey, Ma, what are you doing? Give me back my money.'

'Now you are not depressed.'

'What's that got to do with you taking my money? Can I please have it back?'

'No.' Valda goes back to her mopping.

'Ma, quit fooling. Give me my money! That's all I've got until next week.'

Valda mops in Angelina's direction so she has to move to avoid being washed into the floor.

'Hey, watch the shoes!' she cries. 'Come on, Ma. What are you doing?'

'I cure your depression.' She smiles sweetly. 'You know, when I was a little girl we were very poor. We had no money. We were so poor often we had no food. At night I lay in bed and my stomach would make a noise like it was crying to me. I would—'

'Ma, what has this got to do with my money?'

'*Senti!* Listen. My poor little stomach would cry and I would pick leaves off the trees and chew them, anything to stop the crying in my belly.'

Angelina listens, hands on hips, 'What's the point of all of this, Ma?'

'The point, *stupida*, is that we had the life of a dog, we ate scraps, we worked all day, we were so tired we couldn't sleep at night but we were never *depressed*. We were too poor to have the time to be *depressed*. I make you poor too,' Valda shrugs. 'I save you from depression. Eh! Is nothing, I do it because I love you.' She goes on with her mopping ...

Judy is afraid. She is afraid to say what she feels, to make a noise, as if the walls have ears and she is afraid of who will hear her. She tells Anthony she loves him but even that scares her ...

Graziella's blue eyes are hooded as if they come from deep within her, so deep that she can barely see out from them. She writes the word LOVE in the dirt—and then spits on it ...

I love you now and forever

When Giuseppe was born Valda lost a lot of blood and had to stay in hospital for three weeks. Pino's joy at having a son was replaced by his concern for Valda. Even when she came home she was still pale and cried frequently. Joe was a long thin baby who didn't settle easily. He made little whining noises and fretted if Valda left his sight. The only way he settled was if Valda nursed him. Angelina resented her brother for taking so much of her mother's time. When Valda sat to feed Joe, Angelina climbed onto her mother's lap also, trying to push her brother away. When Joe cried Angelina broke out in a wail twice as loud. She had been fully toilet trained when Joe was born but now she started soiling her pants and wetting the bed.

Pino dreaded going home—one of the two children was always calling or crying for Valda. Pino began going into the guesthouse on weekends. He told Valda he needed to plan menus and experiment with dishes but more often than not it was for the peace and quiet of the empty kitchen. One Sunday, after Pino had spent the morning planning the week's meals and then strolling along the beach in the afternoon, he arrived home to find Valda in tears sitting on the lounge chair nursing Joe on one arm and with Angelina asleep on her lap.

She sobbed when she saw Pino. She was a bad mother, she told him. She was so tired all the time. Pino rocked her gently in his arms, ashamed of how selfish he had been. The next day he left for work early and bought her a present, hoping it would cheer her up. It was a dining room cabinet, as big as their lounge room, and ornately carved from the finest oak. Valda loved it. 'Pino, it's so beautiful. It must have been very expensive.' She imagined it in a big house, its shelves filled with delicate coffee cups and ornaments. She saw it as a good omen that things would start to get better.

And Joe did start feeding better and sleeping more. Angelina learned to open the kitchen cupboards and discovered the vegetable drawers with onions and potatoes. She rolled them around, having races, chasing them—they were a constant source of amusement to her. That summer, Pino bought cured pork and added needles of rosemary and Valda's special chillies. They hung their home-made salamis in the oak cabinet to dry.

Anthony started visiting them. At first, calling in on the way home from school and then riding his bike over on the weekend. He liked being with them. Pino told him stories of his homeland

and Anthony imagined it was his home too. He once asked Pino to teach him Italian and for a whole day Pino spoke only Italian, using gestures to help Anthony understand. 'Antonio, you know what would be very nice to learn? To say "I love you now and forever" to your mamma. It is *"Ti voglio bene, per sempre".*'

'*Ti voglio bene, per sempre,*' Anthony repeated.

When he went home, Anthony found Graziella cooking. He put his arms around her and she frowned slightly with surprise. She was just about to return the hug when Anthony whispered the words Pino had taught him. Graziella gasped. She grabbed her son and hit him across the face again and again. Then she shook him until his head ached. 'Never, never say those words to me,' she screamed. 'Never.' When she let Anthony go he ran to his room, trembling, not understanding what he had done that was so terrible. He picked up his alarm clock and, with a shaking hand, undid the screws. He lay the pieces out neatly on his bed—the cogs, the tiny springs, the miniature pins—memorising how each piece fitted next to the other until the image of his mother and her white rage had blurred away and all that was real were the bits in front of him. Anthony did not go back to the Portellis' the next day, or the next or the one after that. He did not see Valda and Pino until twelve years later when he introduced me to them.

4 Minestrone for attention

Entree   *Losing teeth--Death to your family*

Main course   *In God's hands*

Dessert   *Love is like bread fresh from the oven*

A car honks and I jump in my seat. Where am I? For a moment I am lost. The warmth of the taxi and the gentle hum of the engine had lulled me into sleep. The taxi driver smiles at me from the rear vision mirror. 'You sleep, we still have plenty way to go. I wake you when we there.' He smiles again and I know he is trying to reassure me but I do not want to sleep.

When I sleep I sometimes get lost. Lost in my dreams. Dreams I am always afraid I won't find my way back from. Dreams that are not my dreams at all, but that come from someone else and, somehow, I slip into them. I forget to breathe. This life lifts away from me and I see into another world. I see a woman crying, telling me to sit still, a terracotta water pot on my head, my neck aches ... 'Sit still,' the woman cries, she shakes her hands, her nose is big, her eyes are like pools of mud, my neck aches ... I look down on everything around me remembering the details for eternity, the stone fireplace with the hanging copper pot, roughly plastered wall—I see it all.

I wake, battling for breath. I cough and rasp, greedily sucking onto life. As I breathe, I exhale my dreams.

But Zia Valda breathes them in. She believes them. Life holds no surprises for her because her dreams forewarn her. She says, 'I knew this was going to happen, just last week I dreamt ...' and she then goes on to describe something so obscure that I think it could mean anything.

Like the day the telegram came.

Losing teeth—Death to your family

Valda swears she was waiting for bad news because that night she had dreamt of losing teeth. In her dream she was in church. The tabernacle was covered by a white cloth edged in gold needlework. The priest was standing with his back to the congregation and Valda bowed her head to pray. She opened her mouth and spat her teeth out, one by one onto the mosaic floor; they rolled like tiny pearls. When she woke from the dream she reached for her rose pink rosary beads which were under her pillow and knelt on the floor, fingering them. Her dream had been a sign, an omen. For dreaming of losing teeth meant death to someone in the family. Valda knew her prayers could not stop the death but she prayed for the soul to find peace with ease.

Later that day, as she bathed Joe, there was a knock at the door. A telegram for Pino. 'BAD FIRE STOP REGRETTABLY YOUR MAMMA AND PAPA KILLED STOP DEEPEST SYMPATHIES STOP'

Pino was shattered. He had written to his parents of his plans to bring his wife and children back home. That was why he had worked so hard for the past three years. He had spent extravagantly on Angelina's christening but after Joe was born he was determined to take his family back and had been saving zealously.

It was all little Angelina talked about. 'Backome,' she called it. Pino used his savings now for a single plane ticket home, to bury his parents. It was not how he dreamed it would be.

He brought out his suitcase and stroked the bumpy leather. It would be spring back home, he thought. The tiny white *camomille alpine,* and the pink starry *malve,* would be dotted across the mountain. Pino could not imagine the mountain without his parents. He slept little on the flight and thought flying was like being trapped in a land without time. The sun rose and then rose again, night followed night, he could not eat and refused all the meals. 'Food must be eaten within life,' he said. 'The morning sun calls for the rich smell of coffee and the evening lights crave a warm meal, pasta with a light *sugo,* something of substance, but not too heavy, to ensure a satisfied sleep. I cannot eat when the days and nights have no order.'

When he arrived, Old Man Carluccio's son, Enzo, was waiting for him. Pino recognised nothing as he stared out the car window and nursed his suitcase on his lap, occasionally sniffing the aniseed ring cake Valda had packed for him. She had said the flavour was so pungent it would ward off any evil. But even that was not comforting. He reminded himself he was home. But when he saw the charred remains of his parents' house, he cursed a thousand times a fate that had brought him to this. The home was burned beyond repair and the smell of smoke was thick and terrible.

Pino closed his eyes and tried to imagine what had happened. His parents would have cleaned up from their evening meal. Old Giuseppino always helped Maria dry the dishes. It was an unusually cold spring and so the stove had been left on all night to keep the house warm. Old Giuseppino was fastidious about the stove, that it didn't get too hot, that the fuel was stoked properly so that it burnt efficiently, minimising the smoke. Maria often left her apron dangerously close to the stove and Old Giuseppino had chastised her more than once about this. To Pino he had said, 'Women, they have long hair but no brains.' To which Maria had replied, 'I heard that, old man' (she always called her husband old man), and she scoffed, 'Men, they are no better than donkeys. They like to bray and make a big noise but pat them on the head once and they do anything you tell them.'

Yet for all these times they traded insults, Pino could see it was a game between them and their love could be measured by the passion of their arguments. Most nights, as they sat by the stove, Old Giuseppino would ask Maria's advice on business matters and other issues of the day. He listened to her answers carefully and often Pino heard Old Giuseppino repeat the exact opinion Maria had voiced. However, on this occasion, Pino had believed his mother's carelessness had caused their deaths. They died in bed, overcome by smoke before the flames reached them. The only comfort Pino could find was that they died together.

Everything was gone except Old Giuseppino's wine mug which had been left outside by the back door. It was Old Giuseppino's habit to put the mug out every night to catch the dew. In the morning, he drank the few drops that had collected there, saying this kept a man strong. The mug was shaped like a small jug with a pouring lip and had mountain flowers etched on it.

The whole village came to the funeral. Signora Formichella was there, as she was at every funeral. A chair was placed at the front of the crowd near the gravesite, and she led the wailing. When the coffins were lowered she threw herself on them and screeched, as she always did. It took three men to pull her back and Pino had to marvel at the stamina of the tiny woman who appeared so frail. As Pino sniffed a sprig of rosemary and placed it gently on the coffins, he wondered how he could ever leave now that his parents had joined with the earth.

He stayed with Enzo for ten days. During that time, he walked to the Pit and looked into the darkness, he climbed the mountain and sniffed the last traces of the *Bora*, the winter wind, he went to the *piazza* at night and sang with the old men who hugged him and told him how like his father he had become. They all eyed him with a quiet respect, noted the quality of his clothes, the shine on his shoes. *He was a rich man, yes?* they asked. *Everyone in America was rich, yes?*

And no matter how many times he corrected them, saying he lived in Australia, not America, the two were different countries, not everyone was rich there, it had cost him all his savings to fly over, his wife and two children lived in a small two-roomed flat, he worked two jobs for fourteen hours a day—they did not believe him. They narrowed their eyes and looked with distrust at him, wondering why he would deny his wealth to them, his father's friends. They ordered rounds of drinks and expected him to pay, and when he was gone they spoke of how he had changed, how they had been mistaken, how he was not the man his father had been, how America does that to a man.

Pino walked and searched but each corner he turned led him to something that hadn't been there before, when this had been his home. He felt uncertain when he came to a crossroad, and lost his way often. He wandered into churches but found no peace there and climbed one of the bell towers. He leaned his forehead against the cool stone. The buildings more than anything made him realise how new Australia was, with cities so neat and orderly, as if a mathematician had ruled them up on paper and then looked only at the paper as they were built. But as he looked across the mountain from the bell tower he saw how the buildings grew from the earth. They were as much a part of the land as the mountain, founded on the earth but aspiring to the heavens, spires reaching with impossible tips to touch the sky. The cracked and peeling walls were but the shedding of skin and only added to their beauty. Pino thought of Valda, Angelina and Giuseppe and wanted them close to him.

He arranged for Enzo to lease the land that had been his parents'. He packed his case using his shirts to cushion the mug. It was time to leave.

Upon the death of his parents, Pino inherited some money. It was not a large amount but enough to buy a small house. Two bedrooms with a sleep-out. After the tiny flat it seemed palatial. Valda busied herself with sewing curtains and planting flowers. Pino painted doors on weekends and fixed fence posts. He cooked, he worked, but he did not sleep well at night.

In God's hands

At work Pino oversalted the potatoes and forgot to add sugar to the apple tart. Mr George told him to take some time off but he just shook his head. 'I need to work. It is all I have,' he pleaded. That year Pino lived as a shadow. In his head he functioned normally but in his heart he could not find a way to lead him out of the emptiness. Valda waited up for him at night and put little Joe in his arms, hoping that the soft smell of his sleeping child would instil a sense of life. But Pino smelt nothing. On Sundays, Valda sat Angelina on his lap and asked him to tell them stories of home. She watched him look at Angelina with dull staring eyes as he said he could not remember any. Each morning Valda said the rosary three times, she had done all she could, her husband was in God's hands now.

She began getting headaches. A dull throb that stayed with her from the moment she woke until she slept at night. The doctor prescribed tablets that made her so sleepy she rarely took them. When Valda realised she was pregnant again, she saw it as a sign of hope, and prayed to the Virgin Mother that Pino would also see it that way. But when she told him the news his eyes seemed so distant that she wondered if he had even heard her speak. When he left for the guesthouse that night, she held her head in her hands and pressed her rosary beads so hard against her forehead that they left a mark that took two days to clear. She prayed God had not forsaken her. That night she could no longer stand the pounding in her head. She took three tablets and slept without dreaming.

Minestrone for attention

My mother Maria often told me, 'Worries go down better with soup.' It is easy to cook soup, but to cook good soup, to mix many vegetables and let each hold their own flavour, is an art few understand. The secret is attention. Stir it regularly and let it simmer long, do not over boil and stay attentive.

Soak borlotti beans overnight, drain the water. If you use the water they soak in this causes flatulence. Old Man Carluccio always drank the water he soaked the beans in. He said it kept his vocal chords clear so he could sing in the choir on Sunday but I myself doubt this. True, he did have a wonderful voice but the beans had an unfortunate effect on him. To sit behind him in church was an unfortunate experience and my mother warned me to rinse the beans well before cooking.

Add fresh water to the beans and boil until they are soft. Heat oil in a large heavy pan and fry onion, garlic, parsley, rosemary, carrot, and celery. Let the vegetables be coated in the oil and soften. Add salt and pepper, the boiled borlotti beans and their water, and boil while you sing two rounds of 'Nessun Dorma'. Add the spinach and tomatoes and simmer. In a good minestra the carrots still taste like carrots and the spinach still has the earthy grit of spinach. Stir regularly and watch as the purple water thickens and the bruised broth turns into a wonderfully thick *minestra*.

My mother would make this in winter when there were only a few hours of sunlight each day. We slept long, fourteen hours sometimes, for it was so cold there was little else to do. My mother kept a big black pot simmering on the stove, chopping and adding vegetables, and it never ran dry. The warmest spot in the house was at the base of the stove, nearly under the pot. We dipped our mug into the soup and drank the chunky *minestra* that got thinner as the days got darker and the stores of food began to run low. And just when it was nearly a clear broth, the cold ceased and the sun came out and stayed longer and longer each day and then we drank the clear broth greedily, knowing it meant the end of winter.

PP

'We Italians, we think we know everything,' Pino says as he stirs the soup. 'Sometimes I miss my home so badly I can taste it—in my belly. When I cook, often I see people too scared to eat, too scared to let go and try something new. "Just try," I beg. "Have a taste." But some people pick, pick at the edges like little spoggies, only having nibbles. To fully taste—you need a mouthful, so the teeth can chew and the flavour is released.

'Eh. That is what Valda, my fiery little chilli, asked of me. To bite a mouthful and chew it all. How could I refuse?' ...

Valda dreams of houses—this means she is a good mother. She looks at Angelina, crying because Valda will not let her go out with Darlene. '*Piccolina*,' she says, 'nothing dries quicker than tears. Now go help your father in the kitchen.' ...

Graziella goes to the senior citizens' social programme and plays cards. She sits next to Dot McClosky, a tiny bird-like woman with sharp eyes and nervous hands. Dot likes men and has had three husbands but, as she constantly says to whoever will listen, she is bad luck for men. Her husbands have each died in freakish accidents within three years of marrying her. Since husband number three (John McClosky, an Irishman, who was hit by a truck of Johnnie Walker Scotch Whisky—it had been his favourite drink), she has sworn off men saying she loves them too much to marry any more. Her first husband, an Italian, Luigi Rosella, will always be her one true love.

'You never get over your first love,' she often says after a few sherries.

And to Graziella's continued disgust she speaks a few badly pronounced phrases of Italian. 'Co-me stay?' she says brightly as Graziella glares at her, refusing to answer or even acknowledge that she has understood.

Dot McClosky knows everything about everyone at senior citizens and that is why Graziella sits next to her. To listen to her gossipy chatter, mentally alert for anything that will be useful later on. She tells Graziella about Mrs O'Donahue's daughter Sheila. How her husband has run off with another man and left Sheila, pregnant with their fifth child; and about poor old Mrs Herbert, Mr Herbert's wife. She passed away only last month and Mr Herbert is already back at bingo.

Graziella keeps this information to herself and when she is particularly bored she sits next to Mrs O'Donahue and enquires about Sheila and 'her lovely husband'.

'I met him at the Christmas party last year,' she says. 'A lovely man, you must be so proud to have him as a son-in-law. What was his name again?' she asks as Mrs O'Donahue's lip quivers and her nose begins to water.

Or she sits next to Mr Herbert and remarks what a lovely tie he is wearing. Did his wife pick it out for him? And by the way she hasn't seen Mrs Herbert for a while, how is she getting on?

When Mr Herbert has to be led from the room, wailing for his wife, Dot exclaims, 'Graziella, I'm sure I told you about Flora Herbert passing away.' But Graziella just shrugs and goes back to her card game. Dot feels so sorry for poor Mr Herbert that she thinks if she wasn't so cursed with bad luck she'd be tempted to go over and offer some substantial consolation. As she voices these thoughts out loud, Graziella steals one of Dot's cards to give herself four of a kind and win the game ...

Love is like bread fresh from the oven

Pino arrived home after midnight and left for the building site just before six. Valda slept on, deeply. It rained all morning so Pino was able to leave work much earlier than usual. As he was close to home, he saw his children in the playground. Angelina and little Joe were next to the swings, crying. When they saw him, they ran over, hugging him and shivering from their wet clothes. Pino was bewildered. *Whatever were they doing out in the rain, alone?* He carried them home and called for Valda, who was still asleep in bed. Pino was not a man to lose his temper easily but seeing his children out in the street, in the rain, unleashed a storm in him.

'Valda, Valda,' Pino called as he grabbed her in both arms and shook her until her eyes rolled back and her lids fluttered as she tried to focus. Angelina cried, 'Stop, Papà, you'll hurt Mamma, stop.' Pino saw how frightened his children were and stopped. He hugged them and carried them to the bathroom. 'How would you like a nice warm bath?' he asked, trying to calm the tightness in his voice, the trembling in his hand. 'Now tell me, what were you doing out in the park by yourself?'

Angelina hesitated. 'Well ... Mamma was asleep and Joe wanted a swing so I took him to the park because I know the way (because I'm nearly four but he's only two so he doesn't know much), and then it started to rain and Joe started to cry so loud he hurt my ears and that made me cry and then we saw you—and that's the end of the story.' She smiled up at him, 'Papà, are you mad at us?'

'No, *piccolina*, not you.' He unclenched his fist and stroked Angelina's head. 'But you must promise me you won't go out by yourself again, understand?'

Angelina nodded. 'Promise Papà, cross my heart.'

'Yeah, cross heart,' Joe echoed. Pino smiled and felt the steam on his skin, in his throat. It reminded him of the warmth of bread, fresh from the oven, it reminded him of his love for his family.

He went out to the kitchen. He could hear the children splashing, their voices happy now. This was his family. He realised, almost with surprise, how much he loved them. It was a love that almost hurt. It sat full and heavy in the pit of his stomach, like a big bowl of minestrone.

He noticed the photograph of his mother and father, and the wine mug, and he turned away. Valda walked out from the bedroom, she moved slowly, heavily. She took the flowers that Angelina had picked. They were limp yellow sourgrass and she put them in a vase on the mantel next to the photograph. The clock on the mantel seemed to be ticking louder than usual. 'Valda,' Pino called softly. 'This is no good. This place is no good for us. We will go home, where we belong. Everything will be all right there. It's not your fault ...'

Valda blinked at Pino and tried to clear the thickness in her head. 'What you talking about?' she asked.

Pino went on. 'You are a good mother, don't blame yourself but it is this place. No one can be happy here, it is not our home. You will feel better ...'

Valda stood and walked around the room. Her head felt clearer with each step. She asked Pino again what he was talking about.

'We are going back home, Valda,' said Pino. 'We don't belong here. Nothing here is as good as home. Look at the way they live here, everyone in their own little houses, not talking to each other—we don't even wave to the people across the street. And the way they eat! Pooh! They don't know what good food is. I cook the finest *bistecca* in a drop of oil that has just a hint of basil, the flavour is delicate, light—and they cover it in their tomato sauce that stinks of flies and sugar. They drink sweet sherry with my chicken parmiagano, they send back my platters of mascarpone and gorgonzola cheeses and ask for ice-cream. They *aaah*—' Pino screamed as Valda grabbed the crucifix from the wall and threw it at him. He ducked just in time to avoid being skewered in the eye by Jesus of Nazareth, Carpenter, Messiah and latterday makeshift javelin. Instead, it hit the photograph of his parents and knocked the flowers and the mug over. Valda yelled, 'Forgive me, God, but Jesus understands how *disperata* I am. Let me tell you what it is that makes me feel sick.' She walked over to Pino and poked him on the chest. 'You. You and your moans of going home. It's not this place, it's you.' She grabbed his shoulders and shook him. 'You, you *stupido* man.'

'Me?' Pino echoed. He looked at Valda, wide-eyed and shocked by what she had said. She stared back at him, breathing hard. The clock ticked the seconds by. Gradually, Valda released her grip on Pino's shoulders as she felt her anger melt away. She started to laugh. She started with her donkey *hee hee hee* laugh, then her mouth opened wide, her belly shook, her laughter grew bigger, tears rolled down her cheeks. 'Oh' she gasped between laughs, 'your face, you look just like a little boy. Aaah!' she screamed, laughing louder. 'I wet my pants.' And she ran to the bathroom.

Pino sat. Confused. *Who could understand a woman?*

When Valda came back she sat next to him and reached for his hand. 'You're a good man, Pino, but sometimes you are so *stupido*. You can't see your nose because you're looking for the trees.'

'What do you mean I can't see my nose?' Pino said. 'I always see my nose it's so big ...'

'*Silenzio!* I love you, I love our children but I am going mad being alone day after day with no one else to talk to. You work and work and moan you have lost your home, your family is gone ... Look around you. Your family is here. You don't see us any more. You see only what has gone.' She paused. 'Live with us, Pino. Live with us or go.'

Pino was stunned. He let go of Valda's hand and walked over to the wine mug on the ground. The pouring lip had chipped a bit but other than that it was intact. He set it back on the mantelpiece and bent to pick up the flowers that were barely flowers. They were more a weed really, that dogs pissed on, but the yellow petals seemed to hold the light. The light. It was different here, he thought. It wasn't the gold, yellow light of home, but a brighter, whiter light. Oh it could be harsh at times—it made him squint and search for shade—but the whiteness was glorious on a clear blue day, like a sharp lemon sorbet that sent tingles to your toes.

He looked around the room and felt he was seeing it for the first time; the shiny floor, the polished mantel, the second-hand lounge chair that was all they could afford. Valda had covered it with a crocheted rug to hide the wear in the upholstery. He remembered seeing her nimbly twisting thread and hook late at night to make it. He saw the tiny crisscross stitches in the

72

tablecloth that changed colour every afternoon when the sun's rays slanted through the window.

That night at work he thought about what Valda had said. He stirred the bubbling soup. It was a thin purply colour, the colour of borlotti beans softening and letting go of their dried exterior, releasing their soft fleshy centre. It was not an appetising colour but it was right.

'Live with us Pino, or go. That is what Zia Valda said to me.' Zio Pino shakes his head. 'You know I resigned from the building site the very next day. I had more time to see the children, to play with them. Sometimes we went to the park or caught the tram to the beach and had a picnic. Life was good and I didn't mention going back home again.'

5 Almond biscuits for joy

Antipasto Anthony—Prickling with goosebumps
Judy—Seen clearly
Me as a baby

Main course You are no longer my son

Zio Pino answers all my questions. He likes to talk, to think about life and discuss his thoughts. He tells me what happened, how he felt, what he could smell and I see it all as if I am there with him. When I get lost in dreams and can't breathe he holds me close to him and rubs my back; it is soothing, it helps me come back—whole.

It is not the same with my family. When I wake screaming about the village, the steep narrow streets filled with people all pushing against each other and the tall blonde girl with the glass vial of blood, my mother hits me. She slaps me on the face to bring me back. 'What are you saying? Stop it,' she demands.

'What did I say?' I wheeze as I try to get my breath back.

But she only tells me the truths she is comfortable with, so I doubt her truth. My father isn't a man who is easy to be with. I see Zio and Angelina together—he puts his arm around her shoulders and she slips hers around his waist. Their love is like that, it fits together. My father only touches me on my birthday, then he puts his long thin arms awkwardly around me. They are as hard as sticks against my back. I would like to throw my arms around him, nestle in his chest, but he is hard and bony and holds me at a distance. There is space between us.

Only once, he moved forward, came a step closer. He told me about his mother beating him. I could see the pain in his eyes—he stood so close to me I could feel his breath. 'She hit me,' he said quietly. 'She hit me and hit me and hit me, she couldn't stop.'

'What did you do, what made her so angry?'

He laughed then. A hard ugly laugh that didn't sound at all like him—I have never heard him laugh like that again. He lit a cigarette and blew. The smoke floated all the way to the ceiling. 'What did I do? I told her I loved her.'

I lived with my family for twenty-two years. Yet I never saw my mother without her make-up, without her hair done. I never saw my father be anything other than gentle and sad—I wondered where his ugly laugh had come from.

The only stories I know about my family are those Zio or Zia have told me. Zia said that my father was a saint. That he came directly from God because his goodness surely did not come from his parents. I wonder how he survived living with them? I used to pretend he was a child of a fairytale. His mother was a witch and his father an ugly beast. At the end of the story he fell in love and broke the spell that cursed his family. His mother turned into a princess and his father was a handsome king. That was a long time ago though, before I realised: curses are passed on in families.

I looked at yellowing photographs that my mother kept in a shoebox on the top shelf of the linen cupboard. When no one else was home I arranged them in chronological order and filled in the stories around them.

Anthony—Prickling with goosebumps

Anthony is a solemn boy and he stands out the front of the house. His fingers are awkwardly positioned, as if he were fiddling nervously when the photo was taken. The thumb is curled and hooked around the index finger of the other hand. His little finger juts out at an angle. He is dressed in a cap and winter coat and I notice that behind him the front windows of the house have the curtains drawn ...

(... Their house was always dark and cool. Graziella liked it that way. She said she was sensitive to the light. The front room was her special room where no one else was allowed. There, Graziella burnt dull-coloured candles and sticks, which filled the house with smoky coils. She read books, leather bound with gold-embossed covers. Anthony was a quiet child who moved unnoticed from room to room. He touched things, secretly. He sneaked into the front room and touched the cover of the books, fingered the pages that smelt of pepper and irritated his nose. He ran his hand over the small round table that Graziella covered with unusual things: strands of hair, a fingernail, threads from cloth; her collection spilled onto the floor where she lined up the bottles and containers alongside the wall. A butterfly's wing, a button, a dried flower. Anthony spied on her, watched, while she was in the front room burning her candles and dark smelling sticks. He peeped through the crack in the door but it was terrible to see, and he could not tell if the frenzied whispers she uttered caused her pleasure or extreme pain. Listening to her made him prickle with goosebumps.

At night, Anthony put his pillow over his head to block out the screams and grunts from his parents' bedroom. He found the knife his father slept with and touched the blade, shivering at its sharpness. He touched the silver hand-mirror his mother kept on her dressing table and stared into every morning. He touched his own face, feeling for the resemblance to his parents. He had round brown eyes, not unlike his father's. He had a long straight nose, not unlike his mother's. The crease between his eyebrows was his own. He replaced the mirror, carefully, on the dresser and left the room.)

A school photo shows Anthony at twelve in his posh uniform with the other grammar school boys. Their hair is parted on the left and slicked to the right; they all have their hair done in this way—except Anthony. His wiry curls glisten but defy the hair lotion. They spring untidily over his forehead. His swarthy complexion looks even darker in the grainy photo. His reports tell me he had problems at school. His principal, Mr W. J. Mitchell Esquire wrote:

He has extraordinary mathematical ability, a very good grasp indeed of numerical concepts, but shows little or no real aptitude, and no desire, to succeed in other areas. He is courteous and well-behaved, but this lack of ability makes school life difficult for him. Is English his native tongue? This may be where the problem lies. Speaking frankly, he is what is termed a slow learner. Do not be alarmed by this, I assure you he can lead quite a normal life. I do believe you have a stall at the Central Market? Anthony is a strong boy, quite capable of carrying on the family business, you need have no concerns about that.

(... Anthony liked to fix things. He searched out broken parts and positioned them in his mind before carefully piecing the parts together. He spent all his free time at his desk or out in the workshed. He had no friends and often thought about the Portellis but never dared mention them or go there. His parents had not seen them since Angelina's christening and Anthony had not gone there since his mother had beaten him for speaking Italian. He rode past their flat, saw they had moved, and found their new address, but he never dared to try to see them.)

His last school photo is when he is fifteen. His darkness stands out from all the fair-skinned boys. I think he is handsome ...

(... Anthony was still struggling at school when Guido stepped in to decide his future. They were at the dinner table. Graziella was sniggering at how incompetent the teachers were, how Anthony would go to university and study law or politics and become a man of power, when Guido thumped his hand on the table. 'Enough,' he roared. 'The boy will work for me.' Anthony listened in awe. He couldn't remember the last time he had heard his father speak. Graziella screamed and shouted but to no avail. Guido had decided. Anthony started working with his father the next day.

He had to be up by three every morning to go to market. The work was hard but he worked well, satisfied that it was work he could do. The stars became his morning lights, and he searched them out, making up names for them all. He called the largest, brightest star Portelli and he looked for it every morning as he drove the truck to market.)

The change during the following year is quite remarkable. He is leaning on a car that has headlights like cat's eyes. His lanky frame has neat muscles that cling to it and give it form. His arms have thickened and his chest has filled out. His nose is strangely bent to one side of his face. He has grown a handlebar moustache. He is no longer a boy ...

(... He sneaked out at night to go to the gym and boxed. Men bet money and won when he fought. Often he arrived home just in time to go to work, and a sense of peace stayed with him on those days when he had punched and pounded his way through the night. His nose was broken three times and each time he managed to hide it from Graziella until one day she noticed how crooked it was and wondered when it had grown to be that shape. He liked to drive fast and owned a purple Zephyr that he worked on and added to, and on Saturday nights he drove in illegal drag races.)

Overall, I think he had a death wish but lived, despite his efforts.

I don't think he minded working with Guido. I think he found comfort in the brooding silences, and for the first time a type of companionship grew between them. Graziella would have noticed this. It would have made her sick to her stomach.

Zia said Anthony was 'a ladies' man'. When my mother was not around she told me about him. 'The girls all noticed Antonio, he was so handsome,' she said. She put her hands on her waist and walked around wiggling her hips. Flesh shimmied, she was like a whale. I marvelled at the beauty of someone so at home in their body. 'Tony,' she mimicked as she batted her eyelids and I laughed. 'But,' she sighed, 'he was always so sad. I would see him at the market and he would talk to me if I went up to him but he never came up to me, or came to see Pino at our house like he used to when he was younger. The girls posed when he was near but Antonio did not return their smile. Anyway, the girls never lasted. He broke their hearts and then moved on. When your mother went out with him we all wondered how long it would last. I thought he would never marry.'

Judy——Seen clearly

There are no early photographs of my mother. The earliest one I have is one my father took when they were dating. She is lying across the bonnet of his car on her stomach. Her legs are bent and her feet are crossed at the ankles, pointing into the air. Her face is cupped in her hands, she has blonde waved hair and white bobble earrings. She is staring straight into the camera, her lips slightly apart. She has no make-up on. The photograph is grainy and when I look at it closely I see tiny grey dots. But I have never seen her, my mother, so clearly before ...

(... Judy, orphaned as a baby and raised in foster homes until, at thirteen, she runs away. She looks after herself, tries to make friends, but never quite feels at home. The girls on the switch where she works whisper about her when she walks by with her head in the air. The men all seem to like her, they say, that's because she 'does it'. Judy knows what they say about her and tells herself she doesn't care. When she meets Anthony she likes his darkness—it is exotic and makes her feel special to be seen with him. He takes her photograph one day with a box brownie that he holds at his waist and strains from the neck to look into.

She is surprised.

She knows he loves her then. Someone who wants an image of her forever. She is eternally grateful.)

The next photograph is of Judy and Anthony on their wedding day. Perhaps she was moving as the photograph was taken because her outline is slightly blurred. She is not looking at the camera and has a light-coloured suit on. I notice the tightness around her midriff, the taut lines of the fabric ...

(... She was eight weeks pregnant when they married, a quiet registry office ceremony. Graziella must have been quite relieved. Her daughter-in-law was Australian and she was pregnant—this gave Graziella renewed power. She reasoned with Anthony that he and Judy should live with her. They would save money that way and Graziella could help when the baby came.

Graziella served Judy breakfast in bed, a glass of freshly squeezed lemon juice that was bitter and made Judy's nausea worse but Judy drank it every morning, knowing it pleased Graziella. Graziella made Judy soft boiled eggs and cut the bread into strips to dip into the egg. She told Judy she must eat liver three times a week—it would make her baby strong—and she must drink a glass of stout every night to strengthen the baby's bones. She brought Judy magazines to read, put a stool under her feet, and sponged her back.

In the sixth month of the pregnancy, Graziella took Judy by the hand and led her to the front sitting room. The blinds were drawn and there was only one chair in the room. Graziella motioned for her to sit and she took Judy's wedding ring. She threaded it onto some string and held it over Judy's belly, closing her eyes and moving her lips silently. The ring swung in little circles at first and then back and forth, gaining momentum with each swing. When Graziella opened her eyes the swing was sure and Graziella smiled. She told Judy her baby would be a girl.)

Me as a baby

My father holds me awkwardly in his arms. His elbow looks too big and I look too small. I am tiny in his arms. A bundle of blankets.

There are many photographs of me with Graziella. I do not like to look at those. My breath tightens in my chest and it is hard for me to breathe. I see her pride. The cruel set of her mouth, her eyes shine, even from the photograph. She is triumphant. She holds me as if I am hers.

There is only one photograph of me with my mother. Her outline is fuzzy, as if not quite in focus. She is looking down at me but I am looking away to something not quite in the view of the photograph. It looks like a hand stretched out to me, it is turned upwards, the palm is wrinkled, lined, scarred.

I reach for it as my mother looks down—helpless.

When Judy came home from hospital after I was born, Graziella changed. Changed or just let her true colours show. We all have a colour. My friend Ruby reads auras and she says my colour is a magenta pink that radiates love, but sometimes it changes to a darker shade, the colour of the sky before a fierce dust storm that dries the tear ducts and closes the pores. That is when I feel Graziella in me. Graziella's colour is dull and dark like black, which is no colour really, or maybe grey, with streaks of red for her power.

When Anthony and Guido left for work in the morning, Graziella would take me into her room and lock Judy out, only letting her in when I was crying for a feed. Graziella kept telling Judy she should wean me off the breast, that formula milk would be better for me. Judy must have feared that if she did wean me Graziella would never give me back. Graziella loved me. She rubbed cold-pressed grape seed oil into my skin after my morning bath, she handwashed my clothes in Velvet soap and she carried me, even as I slept. She called me 'her baby' and whispered to me all day long. Her hot breath licked my ear and burned inside my head.

Anthony had no idea what was happening. He was seeing a gentler side to his mother that he had not seen before. Even Guido played with me and it seemed the happy loving family Anthony had always wished for had finally come true. Only Judy was unhappy, crying silently to herself at night as she hugged me to her. And what could she complain about anyway? That her mother-in-law loved her granddaughter too much? Shouldn't she

84

be grateful that Graziella was so willing to help with her baby? These were questions she had no answers to and so she said nothing.

It was my father who made the decision in the end. He was home unexpectedly early one day and found that Graziella had locked Judy out of the house. He was furious. They packed and left that night. Graziella cried and pleaded with them, wailing for her lost child, for me. When that didn't work she turned to cursing. She pointed her fourth finger on her left hand at Judy's stomach and uttered words that were thick with breath. Judy begged her to stop as she fell, crippled with pain. Anthony picked her up and put her in his car, drove off and did not turn back.

We drove around and around that night, not knowing where to go until Anthony remembered someone from long ago. We went to Pino's.

You are no longer my son

Pino hunted in cupboards for a bottle of wine. 'Antonio, this is an occasion, yes? First we celebrate your wedding to this beautiful woman,' he took Judy's hand and kissed it, 'then we celebrate the birth of your beautiful *bambina*,' he took me from Judy's arms and threw me into the air. I hiccupped, not knowing whether to cry or laugh. He did it again and this time I laughed, a delighted squeal. Valda called the children out and introduced them. 'This is Angelina, Guiseppe, Russo and our baby Alessandro.' Anthony offered congratulations. 'Four children, is it that long since I've seen you? I remember Guiseppe being no bigger than our little one, and Angelina,' he sighed as he looked at the young girl. 'I remember your christening. You were so beautiful.' Angelina blushed.

Pino looked proudly at his daughter. 'Aaah, you remember the christening, eh? What a night that was.'

Anthony turned to Russo. 'And what did you say this young fellow's name was?'

Russo answered. 'Russell. I'm Russell,' he said.

'Well, pleased to meet you Russell.'

Valda brought over a tray of almond biscuits. 'When we had Russo,' she explained, 'Pino decided we would stay in Australia, so we thought we should give our baby an Australian name. But,' she smiled at Judy, 'we didn't know any. So, a customer of Pino's, a *professore* at the university, a very intelligent man, he told Pino Russ-ell is a very good Australian name. Only,' she shrugged, 'it's not so easy to say, so we call him Russo.'

Anthony nodded. 'And Alessandro?'

'Oh, well, when Alessandro was born we pick an Italian name again because it's so much easier for us to say, it's much better.'

Judy smiled at Russell. 'How old are you, Russell?'

'I'm eight, how old are you?'

Pino clipped him over the head. '*Basta!* He's a cheeky one that one.'

That night the children slept in the lounge and gave Anthony, Judy and me their room. Pino said we were welcome to stay as long as we needed to but the house was already overcrowded, with six people sharing two bedrooms and a sleep-out. Anthony said we would find somewhere else to go in the morning. But when Anthony went to market the next day Graziella was there waiting for him. 'You no longer work here,' she said. 'You are no longer my son.' Anthony looked to Guido who kept his head down and worked silently moving boxes. Anthony returned to the Portellis'.

He told Pino it was the best thing that could happen to him. It gave him the freedom to try what he had always dreamed of doing. He sold his car and used the money to rent a workshop. He painted a sign on the window, 'Tony's Fix-It Shop' and opened the doors for business. His shop was a success from the day he started. Fixing toasters, irons, watches, even a television set. Anthony was often so absorbed in the problem that he lost all sense of time and arrived home long after dinner.

Judy was very lonely during this time. She wanted to like Valda, she felt she should like her, but she didn't. Valda yelled at the children, sang as she scrubbed, made sucking noises as she ate— everything about her was strong and loud and full of life. She frightened Judy.

Almond biscuits for joy

Italians do not make many sweets. On special occasions and religious days, yes, but usually cheese is best to follow a meal or fruit, fresh from the garden. However, with coffee and good friends, nothing goes better than almond biscuits. They bring joy to the occasion.

With a mortar and pestle grind 400 grams of almonds. In nature, the taste of almonds in any plant is almost always a sure sign of cyanide, poison, death. What better way to be reminded of the joy of life, eh?

Mix the crushed almonds with 4 egg yolks, 400 grams of brown sugar, 250 grams of butter, self-raising flour and a glass of marsala. Pour 2 glasses, one for the mixture and one to sip as you mix the ingredients to a firm dough. Roll it out on a greased tray to about a half a centimetre thickness and decorate with almonds. Bake it slowly while you listen to Act II of Puccini's La Bohème. Especially listen for the joy of the street vendors shouting their wares, Mimi's sweet love

for Rodolfo, the crowd cheering the handsome drum major, and
Musetta with her heart full of mischief.

   Our joy is the light in our life.

                                                              PP

Graziella hates the light. It hurts her eyes and burns her skin. She
keeps the blinds drawn and calls on inner places of darkness ...

Pino stays in Australia because the light is brighter, harsher sometimes but lighter than the light back home ...

Valda prays. 'He is the Way, the Truth and the Light,' she says
...

Judy says she has a light complexion but she dyes her hair blonde
and draws on her light brown eyebrows ...

I look at the scales and eat another chocolate bar—I will never be
lighter ...

6 Baccalà for lost travellers

Appetiser   *If you travel alone you could disappear*

Entree   *Love makes you sick*

Main course   *I want our child to be perfect*

Dessert   *Your family is your family*

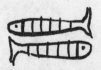

I f you travel alone you could disappear

The day I decided to leave Australia I told Valda first.

'I'm going to Italy, I booked a ticket today.' We were eating lunch, just the two of us. Pino had gone to La Montagna.

'That is wonderful. A holiday is just what you need.' Valda clasped her bosom. 'Who are you going with?'

'No one. I'm going alone.'

'You're going alone? No, no no no, that's too dangerous, a pretty girl like you. They kidnap you, or try to sell you drugs, or,' Valda nodded knowingly, 'they give you drugs to smuggle for them.'

I burst out laughing. 'Zia, you watch too much TV.'

'Aaah, you laugh, but is true. The people in Italy are all scoundrels, just waiting for an innocent *ragazza* like you. You know, Rosa Sauchella went away alone for a week but she was kidnapped and made to work on a ship for five years she only escaped when she jumped overboard at a port but then she hit her head and forgot who she was—even her own fiancé Mackerel Ross-Smith, he was the youngest executive the fish factory ever had. When she met him it all came back but it was too late, Mackerel had married her best friend and Rosa was heartbroken.'

'Rosa Sauchella, I know that name, is she a cousin?'

'No! She's married to Dr Neilson on TV on "Days of the Beautiful People".'

'The soapie?'

'Si. She was a Spanish *principessa* but now she's married to Dr Neilson, only because he tricked her, she thought it was what Mackerel wanted but Mackerel had just told Tyler, his wife that he would divorce her because in his heart he still loved Rosa.'

'Hang on, Zia, what are we talking about here?'

Valda sighed patiently. '*Bella,* please listen. This could happen to you too if you travel alone. Please. Every day I hear people talking about someone they know who went away alone and now they are missing. Just like that,' she clicked her fingers, 'they disappear.'

'Where do you hear this every day? Don't tell me on "Days of the Beautiful People" because that's TV—it's not real.'

'*Bellissima,*' Valda said slowly as if she were talking to a small child. 'On the wireless every day I hear this on 5AW Vincent Cordelli, he's an Italian boy you know, lovely voice, very nice boy, I talked on his show once, did you know that? I know his *nonna* too. She used to shop at the market when I worked there, a beautiful lady, she's got trouble with her hip now ...'

I reached over and kissed Valda on her forehead. 'I do love you, Zia.'

Valda looked surprised. 'Of course you do, *bella,* I love you too.'

I arrive at the airport.

I pay the taxi driver and give him a generous tip. He immediately looks distrustful. I know I have given him too much but I want him to have it. I try to explain this, that it is a gift, but instead I see I have offended him. I wonder if I should offer to take the money back but he drives away before I have the chance.

The airport is humming, like a chorus waiting for the main star to pick up the melody. I stop walking and listen to it: people walking, jostling with bags, trolleys squeaking, feet shuffling against the carpet, children talking, announcements being made, an undercurrent of machinery buzzing in the background.

Zio loves music. He is always whistling or humming or singing, he listens to opera as he cooks. He says he likes the arias the best, the parts where the voice finds its own path and rushes ahead, alone, fearless. 'I can smell the food cooking when I hear this music,' he says.

I like all the sounds jumbled together, in harmony with one another.

I check in and go to the lounge. Among all the grey and blue furnishings I see my parents waiting for me. I see my parents but between seeing them and recognising them there is a gap, a silence. Time is full of gaps that are so minute that they cannot be measured, even by all those sophisticated machines used in the Olympics that measure tenths of hundredths of seconds.

My friend Ruby meditates to music. She listens for the silence, for the moment before the bow glides over the strings, the breath before the note. She says there is a great stillness that we all come from but we can only return to when we truly hear the music so well that we are no longer separate from it—that is where we find the stillness, the gap, between seeing and recognising.

In that moment I see my parents as they really are. It is like seeing a dead body—the essence of who it is, is missing. I see my father like that now. He is a tall man but the curve of his shoulders tells me of his body's defeat. His head hangs, his feet turn outwards, he doesn't know which way to go. My mother is like a chirpy bird. Small, blonde, her blue eyes shadowed by dusky mauve, flawless skin, burgundy lips, tastefully dressed in a cream leisure suit. She is attractive but not beautiful.

Never beautiful.

She sees me as I see her and waves me over.

'Grace,' she calls. 'Over here, Grace.' She calls it out as if announcing me to the world. I go to her and she hugs me lightly, turning her head slightly so she doesn't crush her hair. She smells of strong sickly flowers, I feel nauseous.

Love makes you sick

Every second Sunday my stomach cramped and I would lie in bed quietly crying. 'Do I have to go today?' I'd ask. 'I feel sick.'

'Yes of course you have to go, now stop making a fuss,' Judy would say. Then she would come close to me and whisper, 'Don't be so selfish, think of Anthony. It means a lot to him that you visit his mother, it's only for a couple of hours.'

Every second Sunday I visited Graziella. I was a little fat girl who couldn't breathe and who prayed for Sundays never to come. But I knew her power was stronger than God's. Anthony drove me to her house and left me at the gateway. I never thought of her as Grandmother, but only as Graziella, *strega*, witch. I knew this was true because I found proof of it in the *Encyclopaedia Britannica*. There is a drink called Strega that is said to have been invented many years ago by a coven of witches who met by the banks of a river. They made a magic potion for couples who wished to fall in love, to be together forever. Graziella is Graziella Sabato and the coven of witches are said to have met on the banks of the River Sabato ...

Taller than a man, white hair coiled like a snake and eyes like lollies sucked to milky blue, she looked down her sharp nose, waiting. I dreaded her tight hard mouth touching me, her oily breath condensing on my ear. I wanted to refuse to kiss her. I stood my ground, trying to ignore the cheek before me. But her stare was like a fire licking and pricking and when I could stand it no longer, I lowered my eyes and went to her, knowing I could not escape.

Blood is thicker than water.

I saw Graziella's blood once. Graziella cut herself with the bread knife and her blood was thick and red. The red was so terrible on her pale skin that I shut my eyes. But Graziella made me open them and held her cut hand over my head. 'We are the same blood,' she smiled and I felt the drips lightly trickle onto my head. I knew Graziella was making a spell and didn't move, but that night I rubbed with the scrubbing brush until my scalp burned. As I lay in bed I could still feel the soft trickling drip on my head, Graziella's blood oozing into mine. Then I could not breathe. The doctor said I had asthma. I was to have medication every day, do breathing exercises, swimming, but I knew what it was.

It was Graziella—inside.

She could see inside my head.

'What did you do this week?' she asked.

'Nothing much,' I replied and because I knew what the next question would be I prattled on, 'Ruby got a new skipping rope. She's my best friend at school and she let me use it all recess time.'

'Mmm,' Graziella said. 'I'm sure you would like a new skipping rope.'

'Oh, I don't need one,' I said, clenching my fists so my fingers curled into a tight hard ball and my nails dug into my palms.

'Yes, but yours is old.' Graziella cooed, 'Not as good as a new one. It's not fair some people get everything when they don't even deserve it.'

'I don't mind.'

'You should mind, it's not fair,' Graziella snapped. And then in a calmer voice she went on, 'But the world is like that. An unfair mean place where you can't trust anyone—except family.' And then Graziella asked the question she always asked, 'Have you seen Him this week?' 'Him' was my grandfather, Guido. Graziella always asked me about him and I couldn't lie even though I wanted to.

'Tell me,' Graziella asked. 'Does he still have a whore with him? Is it the one with red hair who looks like a mouse? She can't even wash properly—the clothes are dirty even on the line. Do they give you drinks? Lollies? They put poison in the food, you know.'

'I never eat there, never.'

'Good.' Graziella smiled and opened her jar with the red flowers transfer and gave me a Cherry Ripe. 'Good girl.'

I ripped off the wrapper and bit into the warm softness of the chocolate. 'I don't love him, only you,' I said, and tried to smile but my lips felt tight and wouldn't move. I bit larger pieces of the chocolate, trying to fill my mouth with the thick coating and not let any more words out. I wished I could plug my mouth with the sticky chocolate.

Graziella sneered, 'You say you love me but you visit Him.' Then she started whispering, 'He used to hurt me at night in the dark,' and she gave me more chocolate as she whispered, 'Psst psst psst,' in my ear. I chewed harder, faster, biting larger chunks until my cheeks bulged and hurt they were so stretched. A knock at the door saved me from bursting and Graziella quickly put the chocolate jar away. When Anthony came in I was giddy with relief. Graziella gave me a packet of biscuits to take home.

In the car on the way home Judy asked if I had a nice time. 'Your nanna loves you very much. She has some funny ways and can be difficult but she is family and I know for sure she really loves you.' Judy said this in a thin voice that made me think of daisies dying in a vase, their colour fading and brown creeping in at the edges. I sat quietly, feeling sick and not knowing why— was it the burn of Graziella's breath, her oily skin, or the burden of her love?

I stayed overnight with Graziella once, slept in the same bed as her. I edged as far away as I could from Graziella's cold saggy flesh and lay awake all night, terrified; listening to her moan, fart, mumble in a strange language, her teeth in a jar on the bedside table beside a green lemon and a knife. I saw her in the moonlight.

I prayed to survive the night. To be given another chance, to be sent home again.

Baccalà for lost travellers

We know from the moment we are born that one day we will die. But it is the life lived leading to the death that matters most. The death, pooh, that is the easy part. So it is with baccalà. The cooking is nothing, very quick, but the preparation takes time, care, patience. The preparation is what makes the baccalà so precious.

Take a whole cod fish and soak it for two days. Change the water every 2–3 hours. After two days scratch the sign of the cross on the side and cut a small piece. Eat this raw, washed down with a glass of wine. Now you are ready to cook.

Pour 1 cup of extra-virgin olive oil and add 4 cloves of garlic. Heat the oil. Remove the cloves and place the oil to one side. Steam the *baccalà* with 1 large potato for about two choruses of *'Si. Mi Chiamano Mimi'* and then mix the fish and potato in a blender, picking out the large bones. Add half a cup of chopped parsley, half a cup of thickened cream, 4 cloves of chopped garlic, the heated oil and garlic mix. Blend this very well then add another half cup of cream and another cup of oil. Beat until it is creamy and serve with fresh crusty bread.

The smell of *baccalà* is strong, stronger even, than a mother's love. Cook *baccalà* and you will always find your way home. When my father was called out to help search for lost travellers my mother made *baccalà*, assured this would help him find his way home safely. Aaah! *Baccalà* is truly for travellers. When the cod dies it dies majestically, knowing death is not the end of its journey—just another path.

Salute!

PP

Pino cries big salty tears as he listens to La Stupenda sing *'Mi Chiamano Mimi'*. Her voice on the high notes is like death. Pino is happy to die as he beats the *baccalà* until it is as creamy as silk and the smell is so strong the tip of his nose and ears goes red ...

As Valda spreads the *baccalà* onto her seventh slice of bread she recalls a poem:

Panza Contenti/Cori Clementi
Panza Dijuna/Nenti Pirduna
Contented Belly/A Clement Heart
Empty Belly/Heart of Stone

She goes to church later that day to thank God for her contented belly ...

Anthony sniffs the pungent *baccalà* and lets the smell hit the pit of his stomach. His mouth salivates as Valda spoons the fish onto his plate. For days later, whenever he walks, little gaseous *baccalà* burps surface …

Judy will not let Anthony sleep with her when he has eaten *baccalà*. She says he stinks …

Graziella always stinks—whether she eats *baccalà* or not …

We lived with the Portellis for one crowded year of five children and four adults squeezed into three rooms. Meal times were the worst. The nine of us crammed around the table, bumping elbows and shoulders as we reached for bread to mop up the pasta sauce. The Portellis all tried to talk while they ate, yelling over each other to be heard. The children drank aperitifs before dinner, skinny glasses filled with a clear liquid that burnt and had an after-taste of liquorice. Zio said it stimulated the appetite and helped the digestion.

I want our child to be perfect

Judy refused to let me drink the aperitifs, saying that children should not be allowed to drink alcohol. Valda raised her eyebrows and Pino shrugged and when Judy looked to Anthony for support he also shrugged.

'What harm can it do?' he said. Then he noticed Judy blinking back tears and he added, 'I think Judy's right though, Grace is a bit young for alcohol, let's wait till she reaches her second birthday at least.'

Valda sniffed and filled Alessandro's glass.

Judy said they were irresponsible parents. The children were going to grow up to be alcoholics. 'And they overeat all the time. Pino is a wonderful cook but he uses far too much salt and sugar in what he cooks. No wonder Valda is so overweight. It is a pity really, Pino is such a trim man and Valda is so unattractive. And their children are so badly behaved. I want our children to grow up perfectly,' she told Anthony. That is why I wasn't allowed to call her and Anthony 'mum' or 'dad'. She said I was to feel like an equal with them and that way I would know they respected my feelings and would be encouraged to show them the same respect in return. She said terms such as 'mum' and 'dad' were just authoritarian labels. She even tried to discourage me from calling Pino and Valda, Zio and Zia.

It seemed to me she was against all the words that make a family.

It was while we lived with the Portellis that Graziella's curse on Judy set in. One night after dinner Judy had terrible cramps. They were so painful that she could not walk and Anthony had to carry her to bed. She refused to see a doctor and Valda sat by her side all night sponging her forehead. Valda knew something was seriously wrong for she had dreamed of Judy sitting very still in a room surrounded by growling, guttural noises. Valda did not know what this meant but she did know it was not good for Judy. She prayed for Judy every day and tried to be extra quiet around the house. When she was about to yell at the children she stopped herself and went over to them and slapped them on the head instead. 'Ow, what's that for?' they cried and she would hiss her reply. 'Shshshsh! Aunty Judy is not well.'

Judy stayed in bed for the week. The nausea came and went at various times but by the end of the week she believed it was passing—then the bleeding started. That was when Valda knew for sure. She told Anthony he must take Judy to the hospital. That's when they found out she had been pregnant but was miscarrying and there was nothing the doctors could do to stop it. At midnight that night she was rushed into surgery. No one would speak to Anthony and so he waited, wringing his hands and holding his head, wishing of all the things he could fix that there was some way he could fix this. In the early hours of the morning a gowned doctor with a tired face told him everything was all right. The danger had passed and although there was some risk of infection during the next twenty-four hours, the worst was over. After the miscarriage Judy had haemorrhaged, and nearly died. It was unlikely she could have more children but at least she had one. The doctor put his hand on Anthony's shoulder. 'Be thankful for small mercies,' he said.

When I was growing up Judy often cried. I could see the shadow of her dead baby cloud her face on those days when she'd weep, arms wrapped around her empty womb. Sometimes I thought she would die from the tears. Can a person die from tears? I believe so. The tears create a hollowness so vast that you can see it in their eyes—like a great emptiness, it swallows them.

Judy's outline blurred even more as the years went on. She refused to have her photograph taken because then she could not deny that she was fading. Her body was thin, small folds paunching at the centre. Every wrinkled fold reminded her of the greatness she had once had. When she had been drinking and her voice was thick with alcohol and her words slurred, she forgot her fear of being heard and talked about how she felt when she was pregnant.

How her skin had been a perfect fit, tight and ripe. Her breasts had hung, heavy, casting shadows on her swollen belly curving downwards, exotic. Clothed, she was huge, cumbersome, but naked she was a feast of flesh. When she told me this I stood back, separate, and tried to concentrate on her faint outline in the mirror.

I knew I could not help my mother.

Your family is your family

We moved out of the Portellis' after a year. Anthony's fix-it shop had gone so well that he looked around for a larger site. He found one with a large shopfront and small live-in area out the back: a kitchen, lounge, one large bedroom that could easily be partitioned off into two rooms, and a laundry, bathroom and toilet off a hallway that led into the shop. Judy thought it was a palace. She sat in the quiet lounge far away from the noise and life of the Portellis and wondered if she would ever recover.

During the day she often went into the shop, watching Anthony work, touching his hair as if reassuring herself that he was real. At night, she always held on to him, clinging as they lay in bed, her nails deep in his flesh. I missed the company of the other children and although Anthony took me to visit the Portellis often, I always cried when it was time to leave.

Anthony had not seen Graziella since the night he and Judy had left her house. He heard from various people that Guido had sold his stall at the market. He told Pino and Valda, 'I have no wish to ever see my parents again. If they died it would not bother me. They are already dead to me.'

But Valda chastised him when he said this. 'Antonio,' she said as she blessed herself, 'do not speak such words, God will punish you for saying them.'

'But Valda, whether I say them or not it's true, it's how I feel. They hurt my family.' But again, Valda shook her head. 'Antonio,' she said sadly, 'they are your family, you can never deny that. Your family is your family.'

Valda called into Anthony's shop one Tuesday morning on her way home from the market. She was laden with string bags and breadsticks. She wondered if Anthony had heard the rumour? It was said that Graziella had left Guido. She had walked away from the house with no suitcases or belongings. It was said she had cursed Guido. 'Your eyes will close but you will not sleep,' she had called. Since then, no one had seen Graziella, and Guido stayed shut up in his house all day.

When Anthony repeated this story to Judy she begged him to go and find out what was happening. The thought of Graziella and her searing words made Judy fearful for us all. 'You must make peace with your mother, you must,' she pleaded. Anthony finally did go and visit his father, who confirmed what Valda had said. Graziella had left. He had no idea where she had gone but, he whispered, she was a witch. He could feel her eyes watching him all the time. Anthony felt it too, and when he went into his father's back yard the hairs stood up on his neck. It took him nearly a year to work it out. He was at the back of his father's one day and he thought he saw an eye through a hole in the fence. He called out and ran to the fence just in time to see a woman disappear inside a house. It was his mother. She had rented the house behind his father's.

Anthony made enquiries at the Housing Commission, which leased out the house. The clerk was very helpful. Yes, he knew Mrs Sabato well, he said. A lovely lady, very tall and fair, she brought biscuits, soft buttery ones, every fortnight when she paid the rent. She was a widow and had specifically asked for the house that backed onto her brother-in-law's property, a Mr Guido

Sabato. She said it had been her husband's dying wish that she stay near his brother and luckily for her, a week after she applied for the house the woman who had been living there disappeared. 'Funny business that,' he said. 'The old lady never showed up again, not even to collect her things. It makes you wonder about some people. Anyway it meant Mrs Sabato was able to move in almost immediately.'

Anthony went to see her but she would not even open the door. She called through the screen. She was happy where she was, she couldn't take living with Guido any more. She just wanted to be left in peace. 'Left in peace,' Anthony scoffed, 'then why rent the house behind Dad's?' Graziella refused to answer.

He asked if she wanted him to visit her. 'I'll bring Judy and Grace,' he offered. But she said she would not have Judy in her house.

Anthony would never have agreed but it was Judy who insisted I meet with Graziella regularly. In the end, it was decided. I would visit her every fortnight and in return she had to promise not to say anything bad about my mother. And that is what happened for the next thirteen years. Every second Sunday I visited her. Anthony thought he had accomplished something with this. He thought knowing Graziella loved me would give me the sense of family that he had missed.

My poor stupid father.

7

to forget troubles eat fritelle

Appetiser   *A king never leaves his castle*

Entree   *God and garlic*

Main course   *See less of you next week*

Dessert   *Sleeping sounds*

'Grandma.' A small girl runs towards a smartly dressed older woman. I watch as the two hug.

I always wanted a grandmother. I remember how friends at school spoke about their grandparents. They were like co-conspirators, they gave extravagant presents and were more understanding than parents. I felt cheated—instead of grandparents I got Graziella and Guido.

A king never leaves his castle

Guido ran advertisements in the personal columns. 'Retired European Businessman seeks female company. Free board in return for light household duties. Apply to Guido Sabato ...'

Within a month of Graziella leaving he had a Dutch woman, Ingrid, living with him. She was the first of many. A gentle woman with soft blonde hair and a soft lilting voice to match.

Others came, usually widowed women of ethnic origin who didn't want to be a burden on their family. Women who were used to having a man around to depend on, to take care of, women who wanted some companionship. Betty was English; Magda—Polish; Anna—Ukrainian. It was the German woman, Heidi, who gave Guido a black eye when she left. And they did all leave. No one lasted longer than three months. Each told Anthony the same story. They were sorry to go but they could not stay any longer—Guido was a mad man. He took all their pension money as board yet expected them to cook and clean and sleep with him. He slept with a knife and was insanely jealous, he was tormented by visions and voices not of this world. Guido did not seem to feel sorry when they left, he just ran his ad again. When Anthony and I visited him he would look at me from his good eye and say, 'Are you here about the ad?'

Anthony would groan in frustration, his shoulders slumping forward even more. 'Dad, it's Grace, your granddaughter.'

'Pity,' Guido would shrug, 'she looks strong.'

He became obsessed with the idea of building an armour and he rang our house at all hours demanding Anthony help him. He needed protection, he said, although Anthony had no idea what Guido wanted to be protected from. Guido worked in his lounge room, rather than the workshed, because 'it was further away from prying eyes', he said. He made shields of all shapes and sizes, cutting them out of old rubbish tin lids. He made helmets, using buckets, old tyres and foam packaging. The lounge room was filled with junk. Anthony tried to clear it all away several times but Guido would not let him. 'Dad, this place is a pig sty. Why don't you at least come and stay with us for a couple of days and I'll clean things up here. I'll give it a fresh coat of paint and—'

'No!' Guido thumped his fist against the wall. 'I am the king. The king never leaves the castle.' He looked at me. 'Remember that. Or the soldiers will sneak up behind you. The minute I am out the door they will be here.' He stared into Anthony's eyes through the eye slit in his helmet and tapped his breastplate which was made from flattened aluminium cans welded together. 'I outsmart them all though. When they come through the door—I'll be here, ready for them.'

Anthony looked at his father and his shoulders seemed to hang forwards even more than usual. 'Just come over for a meal, Dad.'

'No, no no no no. You want me out of the castle so you can rob the treasure.'

'What treasure, Dad? The place is full of junk and it's falling down, you won't let me paint it or do anything to it. I think you've got rats in the roof, it stinks.'

'Aaah, you say that but you're in with the enemy. You'll plant little wires that have ears and eyes and spy on me. I know these things can be done—I watch "Beyond 2000".'

Anthony gave up.

So Guido stayed home. He used to call to people walking by his house to ring his son for him. At odd hours Anthony got phone calls from strangers saying they were ringing on behalf of his father and Anthony would rush there thinking it was some type of emergency only to find that Guido had an idea to build a force field around the house and wanted Anthony's opinion of it.

'Dad, why don't you call me, on the telephone?'

But Guido whispered conspiratorially, 'I don't trust wires, you never know who is listening. Eh?' He tapped his nose. 'It is safer this way.'

I didn't really mind Guido so much. I just hated being around when he ate. He ate with his arm spread across the front of his plate and his head bent over so his face was nearly touching the food. He shovelled mouthful after mouthful in, never stopping until the plate was empty. I wondered how he could breathe. Often, I'm sure he nearly choked, he coughed and spat bits of food out yet even then he didn't pause but ate right through it. Ruby said it was because he died of starvation in another life and had to fight for every morsel he ate. That was the karma he brought with him to this life. That scared me so much I couldn't sleep for a week. I felt burdened enough with this life with a mother who was fading, a father who couldn't talk to me, a grandmother who was a witch and a grandfather who was a wacko. How could I cope with the burden of another life as well?

To forget troubles eat fritelle

Fritelle have such a light sweet taste that you can forget who you are when you eat them. The sweetness has wings that carry you away, as far away as the moon, and anything that has been troubling you will quickly be forgotten. My mother made these sweets at Easter, for new life, and hope, and also because there was a full moon. Only make fritelle when the moon is full otherwise they do not cook to be round in shape.

In a bowl mix milk, sugar, 2 eggs, flour, vanilla and a handful of sultanas. The mixture must be as thick as the fog on a winter's day. Heat a small deep saucepan with oil and drop a teaspoonful of the mixture in. It will rise to the top and turn itself over when the underside is cooked. Remove from the oil and drain on some absorbent paper.

My mother used to cook these one at a time but I put four or five in at once and find they still cook well. Let them cool and then sprinkle with castor sugar. When you bite into them you will see they are as white as the moon on a clear night.

PP

On full moon nights Graziella slips off her nightgown and stands outside on the grass. The pearly lustre opens her skin. She kneels and digs her fingers into the ground, cool dirt under her fingertips, her white hair hanging around her shoulders. She spits—a gob of spittle that shines like silver. She whispers as the silver, the dirt, and the moonlight mingle. 'Psst psst psst,' she says. She feels power surge through her and knows she is strong, stronger than any man. She raises the hat pin with the pearl end that looks like a miniature moon orb and pricks it deep into her ring finger. The blood drips onto the dirt ...

On full moon nights Pino mixes the *fritelle*. Beats the mixture with a wooden spoon—*shshshlap shshshlap shshshlap*. As they fry and golden flecks of oil spit, he sings '*Nessun Dorma*' ...

On full moon nights Guido puts on his armour and sits by the door of the front room. He is the king, he is ready ...

On full moon nights Valda smokes in the bathroom. She locks the bathroom door, and even though Pino is at work and the children are all asleep, she feels better with the door locked, sure that no one can see her. She opens the window wide and lights a cigarette. Her blood pressure is high and the doctor has warned her to start watching her diet, drink less coffee and give up smoking. Valda has feigned innocence at this. She doesn't smoke, she says, everyone knows that. How can she give up something she doesn't do? And she doesn't smoke, well, not really, well, she doesn't smoke in front of anyone—except for Patty and so that hardly counts as smoking at all, really.

She sucks and blows. All day she has been waiting for this moment. As she blows the smoke out the window she looks up and sees the moon as round and full as *frittoli* ...

On full moon nights Judy cannot sleep. She tosses and turns and clings to Anthony. 'Hold me, hold me,' she whispers. But no matter how tightly he hugs she does not feel he is any closer ...

ᕪ

'It's such a long way from home,' Judy pouts. 'Why not go for a holiday on the Gold Coast? Get some sun, relax on a beach? Why halfway across the world?' She is showing off, playing concerned mother. I sigh loudly, this is a conversation we have had many times. 'Let's go to the coffee shop,' I say, trying to change the subject.

'*Grazie a Dio*, there she is!' I hear the shriek. 'Grrruss, Grrruss.' It is Zia Valda. She comes running over, red in the face, panting for breath. '*Bella*, I thought we were too late.' She throws her arms around me and kisses me, hard and wetly on both cheeks.

Zia has none of the regal elegance that Zio Pino has. She is fat. Big and cushiony. Her black hair is plaited and pinned around her head with wispy bits that stick out like a fuzzy halo. She is an Angel. An Angel in black. Angel Valda. Zia says she is interested in people and likes to listen but she interrupts all the time, adding things totally unrelated to what you were talking about. She is constantly using other people to talk to Zio, because she refuses to talk to him directly any more, since the restaurant.

She rolls her Rrrs and purrs my name like a satisfied cat. She has always liked me because I eat everything. Zia is big on eating and it pleases her to see people eat, especially children. As a child she was often hungry and she has a saying, 'A stomach full of food is the stomach of a rich person.'

God and garlic

'See,' Valda told her children when I visited them, 'Grrruss eats so well that is why she will grow beautiful.'

Russell looked me over. 'Yeah, and fat.' Valda leaned over the table and slapped him across the head.

'*Basta*, Russo. Look,' she went on, 'she is already a beautiful girl.' She pinched my cheeks. Then she stood with her hands folded and watched her children with their *baccalà*. They were not allowed to leave the table until they had eaten it all. Russell sneered and blew me a kiss when his mother's back was turned. Joe pinched my leg hard and Alessandro leaned forward and hissed, 'Why'd yer have to eat the *baccalà*? It stinks.'

I remember them all staring at me. They were the ones I loved the most, the ones I wanted to be a part of—and they hated me. All because I ate the *baccalà*. I felt my chest tighten and the blood drain from my head. I gasped for air, I could feel Graziella's breath burning my ear—I began to drown.

When I came home from hospital I had to rest. My little body had been through a lot, the doctors said. The asthma attack was near fatal. I had stopped breathing and it was only Alessandro's quick thinking that had saved me. When he came to visit me he had smiled a lot and stared. He told me he had learnt mouth-to-mouth resuscitation at the lifesaving club. He had practised many times but only on a mannequin. He seemed to want to say more, but didn't. Valda brought me almond biscuits and *fritelle*, and when the doctors weren't looking she rubbed crushed garlic on my chest while she said a prayer. She said with God and garlic you could cure all ills.

'Grrruss, call that *stupido* man, he's over the other side.' I see Zio squinting, scanning the faces near him. He is short sighted and refuses to wear glasses, saying they make him look like an old man. I go over to him and when he hugs me I feel I have found a place I never want to move from. '*Piccolina*,' he says. He links his arm in mine and we walk over to Zia, Judy and Anthony. 'Oh, I am so glad we have not missed you, of course we would have been much earlier but your Zia Valda was fussing as usual—'

'Oh *Dio*,' Zia says loudly. 'That man has fantasies. Tell him I was ready on time but who took the wrong turn when I told them the right way? Eh?' Zia rolls her eyes. '*Che miseria*,' she mutters. 'What I put up with, you would not believe.'

We sit at a table and Anthony orders coffees for everyone, except Judy. She has lemon tea. She is watching her weight, she says pointedly, looking at Zia.

Watching her weight do what? I think. Judy diets all the time. She is a slim woman but she has a need for perfection. And I am not perfect. I don't fit her image of what the perfect daughter should look like. I am too fleshy, too real and that frightens her. I was a chubby baby who grew into a fat girl and an even fatter teenager. Judy kept waiting for me to transform, you know the saying, inside every fat girl is a thin one just waiting to get out? But at sixteen I still showed no signs of slimming down. My thighs were heavy and my midriff bulged, my arms were soft and flabby and I had a double chin. People said that I was a happy girl but Judy told Anthony she knew they only said this because I was fat. 'Fat and jolly,' she said. 'People always think the two go together.' The more concerned Judy was about my weight the more I ate. I was often out of breath and the doctors said I should exercise more but when I did I had to stop in order to breathe. After countless visits to dietitians Judy booked me into Weight Watchers, Monday nights at the RSL hall.

See less of you next week

The hall had a bleary-eyed beer smell. The carpet was royal blue, threadbare at the edges, and dead moths adorned the window sill. The president was a big fat woman, May, and the secretary, a younger woman, Dana, who was tall and quite noble looking. Dana read the minutes from the last meeting and then everyone 'weighed in'. There were about twelve people usually and they all stood around and offered encouragement to each other.

'Well done, love, lost a kilo this week didja?'

May weighed in last of all, shamefaced but smiling. 'Don't think I want to do this tonight,' she said. 'It's been a bad week for dieting.'

She had gained two kilos.

She introduced me to everyone and gave me a recipe and progress book. 'For the first week record everything that goes into your mouth in the book. Drinks and all.' Then the meeting began. They talked about how the week had been. May told about the party they went to for her husband's boss's retirement. 'I had two chocolate mousses,' she confessed. The others nodded sympathetically.

Then Dana spoke. 'Well, just because you've fallen off the wagon once doesn't mean you've failed. Treat each day as a new start. Remember, it's only one day at a time you have to get through. One meal at a time.'

Everyone nodded, someone murmured, 'You tell 'em.'

'Come on, let's all say it together,' Dana called.

They all joined in with the slogans:

> 'Treat each day as a new start.'
> 'It's only one day at a time I have to get through.'
> 'One meal at a time ...'

I repeated them with the others. I quite enjoyed the meeting—it reminded me of going to church with Valda. It all ended at ten p.m. Judy was waiting for me out the front. As I walked out people called to each other, 'See less of you next week.'

'How did it go?' Judy asked.

'Great, they were all really nice. I think it will work out fine. I've got this recipe sheet I have to follow for the next week and I have to write down all my meals.' I felt excited about the prospect of losing weight—it would be nice to wear jeans and feel comfortable in them. 'I'm really glad I went, Mum.' Judy looked surprised when I said that and smiled back.

The next morning I had a half slice of wholemeal toast and a poached egg for breakfast.

'Have some orange juice,' Judy offered.

'No, I'm full.'

'Here's your lunch, a tuna sandwich and an apple. Are you sure that's enough?' Judy asked.

I felt great. I stuck to my diet all day. But I guess I should have known. Hope is cruel, evil, it plants the seed of despair. That night as I slept and slipped into another world I saw the vial of blood, the saint's blood: the luck of the village depended on the saint's blood liquefying ... the tall girl placed the vial carefully on the altar ... the altar boy had curly black hair and a smile I had seen before ...

I saw Graziella the next day. She was waiting for me as I came home from school.

'Grace,' she called. 'I am on my way home from bingo, I'll give you a lift. Did you have a good day?'

'Yes, it was fine.'

'What did you do?'

'Oh, nothing much.'

'Well, tell me,' she insisted.

'Mmm, there's really not much to tell …'

'Are you hungry? I've got some Mint Slice biscuits in my bag, have some.'

I started to refuse but then it seemed easier just to take one. It was a distraction, it calmed the nervousness I felt at being around Graziella. As I bit and chewed I remembered I was safe when my mouth was full. I ate one, two, three, before I even remembered the diet. Graziella swerved to miss a truck that had braked suddenly in front of her. She yelled abuse at the driver who raised his hand in a friendly gesture.

'Ignorant idiot, shouldn't be on the road,' she muttered. By the time we reached home I had finished the packet. Graziella smiled. 'I'm glad you like those, I'll get you some more next time,' and she drove off without indicating. I felt sick and prayed Graziella would have a fatal accident on the way home.

When I went back to Weight Watchers the following week I was genuinely disappointed. I had eaten all the right foods, had written them down to prove it. What I hadn't written down were the times I didn't like to think about, the packet of biscuits with Graziella, the bag of chocolate bars in my socks drawer that I ate on Saturday night when I was thinking about going to Graziella's the next day, the fish and chips Graziella bought me on Sunday night along with the potato fritters and Chiko roll. I had not gained weight but I had not lost any. May smiled encouragement, 'Don't worry, stick to the sensible eating programme, it often takes time but I guarantee, when it happens, the weight will just fall off.'

The first few days after the meeting were fine, with May's motivational speech still ringing in my ears, but from the third or fourth day it was like I was running on ice, postponing the inevitable. Somewhere along the way someone would offer me something and I would accept and have it eaten before I even realised it. It was the realisation that killed me, not the act. On realising what I had done it was like a floodgate opened and the tide of my hunger poured out. I became almost frantic looking for food, anything to stuff into my mouth.

So I stopped going to the meetings.

When Judy dropped me off on Mondays I would stand out the front of the RSL club and wave goodbye, making sure Judy had turned the corner before running across to the fish and chip shop and spending my session money on a hamburger with the lot and minimum chips. I also became expert at inventing fake events: 'Last night May organised an all-day trip to the museum. It's to recognise there are fun things to do that don't involve food,' I lied. I spent the day having lunch, four in fact, at four different places.

For a year I kept up the pretence of attending Weight Watchers. Judy weighed and measured all my meals and ate the same portions as me to offer moral support, she lost three kilos while I gained five. It all came to an end one day when Judy cleaned out my cupboard and found the chocolate wrappers and biscuit papers. 'You've been lying to me,' she said. I couldn't even begin to tell her what had happened so I didn't say anything, just stood dumbly while she looked at me accusingly and then she whispered, 'You're just like your grandmother.' When Anthony came home Judy cried, dabbing at her eyes so as not to smudge her make-up. 'That girl is a malicious little witch, she does everything she can to hurt me.' Judy was so upset by my defiance she complained her headaches were worse than ever and she needed to get away. She bought two tickets to Fiji and told Anthony they were going away, just the two of them. I was to stay with Graziella. 'See how you like that,' Judy snarled at me when Anthony was out of the room.

Sleeping sounds

Graziella told me she did not dream. But I watched as she slept. She moaned and cursed and mumbled words that were not words. When she woke I asked if she had had a bad dream.

'I do not dream,' Graziella said as she squeezed her lemon juice and drank it and then rubbed the lemon half on the scar along her ring finger.

'But I heard you ... say things.'

'What things?' Graziella grabbed my arm and her fingers dug deep. I bit my lip trying not to cry.

'You said ... things ... words ...'

'What words?'

'Not words. I don't know. Like ... another language ...'

Graziella scoffed. 'Sleeping sounds, nothing really.'

She released her hold on my arm—it left a bright red welt.

'Come, let's have breakfast,' she said.

That night, as Graziella began to moan and call out again I hid my head under the covers and rubbed the scar on my arm.

8

Caffè espresso only

Antipasto Saint Anthony--Patron saint of lost things

Main course La Montagna

When the coffee comes Zio wrinkles his nose in distaste as he sips. 'Pooh! Is not fresh coffee.'

'Eh, God, if he wants fresh coffee tell him to make it himself-- that is the only way to get it,' Zia says. 'Nobody can make *caffè* like the Italians, is true eh?' She looks at us and shrugs. 'When God wanted a cup of coffee--he made Italy.'

'Eh,' Zio interrupts, 'when God wanted good food he made Italy, *non è vero?*'

Zio Pino is not an overly religious man. Of God he says, 'I believe the words my papà told me. He said, "Your family should be your religion".' But Zio's decision to start his own restaurant came about because, as he says, he felt the breath of God warm through him.

Saint Anthony—Patron saint of lost things

It was eight years after the death of his parents that Pino bought his restaurant. He had woken the morning of the anniversary to hear the birds singing and see the liquidambar tree a kaleidoscope of colours as the sun rose. His heart felt light as Alessandro ran into bed with them. He looked at Valda, snoring lightly, and hugged his son. Then he remembered the date and heaviness cloaked him. He thought he remembered his parents so clearly, yet sometimes he forgot what his father's voice sounded like, or how his mother's hands felt when they stroked his brow to sleep and, try as he might, he could not remember the smell of them.

They went to church that morning and as he knelt to pray he tried to feel God. Valda talked to God all the time and he envied her the peace it seemed to bring her. He had hoped his love for her and their children would be enough, but it was not. When he cooked, sometimes, there was something else—intangible—so elusive that he could not honestly say he felt it—but he did smell it.

As he waved his nose over a pungent pot of *baccalà* he was transported to another place, another time and he knew he was home. Although he had not slipped back to the despair he had felt immediately after his parents' death, he felt incomplete. Something was lost and he did not know where to begin to look for it. Valda prayed to Saint Anthony, patron saint of lost property, when she lost things. He was her favourite saint and she was always calling on him to find her keys, her rosary beads, her rings after she had taken them off to scrub the toilet. When she found the objects, as she always did, whether it was that day or the next week, she gave thanks to Saint Anthony, telling whoever would listen, 'I knew he would find it for me. *Grazie, San Antonio, grazie.*'

Pino tried that now. He concentrated on the brown-robed statue to the side of the altar. He stared into the effeminate face with the wry smile and bared his soul. He had lost something, something precious. It was more than the loss of his parents. He had lost a sense of who he was—could Saint Anthony help him? The wry smile seemed to mock him and after a while Pino could not bear to look into the face any longer and he lowered his eyes, ashamed he did not believe. He knew he was lost.

As he walked home with Valda and the children, Pino wondered about his grief. He watched the autumn leaves pirouette to safety and wished his grief would fall as lightly from him. They walked along Beach Road past the grocery store, the Commonwealth Bank, and Yanni's Fish and Chip Shop. Next to Yanni's was the old church. It had been empty for two years and the parish had recently received permission to sell the building. A new church had been built—a large angular building decorated in pastel pinks and muted greys. Pino preferred the old church. It was a blue-stone building with a pointy, shingled roof and a spire that reached up to an impossible point. It had always reminded Pino of something far away …

He stopped and looked at the old church and let himself be carried away. Later, he said he felt God's breath warm through him. Valda called him and he shook his head to clear his thoughts but the warmth, and the memory of that warmth, stayed with him. He said nothing to Valda about it but went back to the church later that day and made a note of the estate agent's phone number. Two days later a courier came to the door with some papers. He trembled as he signed them, not believing he had come this far. Now all he had to do was tell Valda. He called in sick at work, the first time in seventeen years. He rang Vincenzo and Carmella and asked them to come over and mind the children, he told Valda to get dressed, he was taking her out.

Valda was astonished.

'Pino, tell me what is going on?' But he would not say. They walked down Beach Road where Pino went into Yanni's and came out with some chips and scallops. They walked to the beach front and Pino spread out a rug and set out two glasses and a bottle of wine. 'Pino, you are driving me mad. Tell me, what is all this about?' Valda laughed, delighted with the intrigue of it all.

Pino shook his head. '*Basta*. Before all else—comes food.' He clinked his glass against hers and ate a chip. 'You know, there is nowhere here to buy a decent meal,' he said as he fed the chips to the seagulls.

'Eh,' Valda shrugged between mouthfuls, 'if you want a decent meal you cook it yourself.'

'Not any more,' Pino said triumphantly.

'So what's all this?' she sniffed.

'Today I buy a restaurant.'

'A what?'

'A restaurant. Today the papers come. It is mine, ours.'

'A restaurant? Where?' Valda's mind was racing. It was a wonderful idea—Pino could cook and he would be happy. She knew he had been unhappy. Sometimes in his sleep he sobbed so hard it shook the bed and then she held him and crooned softly in his ear until it passed and he slept soundly again. When he cooked he was at peace. A restaurant, she thought, she could help, greet the customers, take their orders. It would be a big success. People would come from all over town to eat there.

'Where is it?' she asked,

'Next to Yanni's.'

'Where? Next to Yanni's is the old church.'

'*Si*, that's it.'

She thought she'd heard wrongly.

'A church? The old church next to Yanni's is the restaurant we buy?'

'*Si*.' Pino kissed her on the mouth, 'I am going to turn it into a restaurant where I cook only the best food, the most exquisite ...'

'Wait, you buy the church?'

'*Si* ...'

'To make a restaurant?'

'*Si*, I will paint it ...'

'What? Are you *stupido*?' Valda stood up. 'You can't have people eating in a church.'

'*Perché?*'

'*Mamma mia*,' Valda crossed herself. 'It's a sin that's why not. It's against God. I never heard anything so stupid. To eat in a church! You offend Jesus. *Madonna*! And what you mean we buy it? How did we buy it?'

He told Valda how he had used the money they had been saving for a house as a deposit—the church, as of two o'clock that day, was officially theirs.

For once in her life, Valda was speechless. She had wanted to buy a house, have a garden with some flowers, a kitchen with cafe curtains like she saw through the windows of the houses she passed as she walked to the shops. She wanted a clothesline in the back yard and a carport—although they didn't have a car. She didn't want a church. It was sacrilegious. Pino grabbed her hand and said, 'Valda, even Jesus had to eat. If he thought that Jewish fish was good, wait until he smells my *pesce spada con patate*. I want to give people something to put under their teeth ...'

Valda hit him on the head.

'I knew this was going to happen. *Mamma mia*, I knew it.' She shook her hands. 'I had a dream last night I held a baby in my arms, a beautiful little baby all soft and chubby but when I unwrapped the blankets, my God,' she beat her chest, 'it had no face. Pino, it had no eyes or nose or mouth, nothing! Completely blank. Oh *Dio, Dio, Dio*, don't you understand?'

Pino shook his head. Did this mean Valda was pregnant again?

'That baby, Pino, it was you.'

'How do you know if it had no face?'

'*Che miseria*, it was you, believe me, I know. If you buy a church and make a restaurant in it, you commit a very grave sin. You will be like that baby, you will lose face.'

'*Beh*, Valda, what does this mean?'

'Pino, I cannot let you do this. God will punish you for your disrespect. I will pray for your soul but I will not speak to the devil. Until you have got rid of that ... that ... sin, I will not speak to you.' She walked back home.

She did not speak to Pino again.

She started wearing black and when people asked who she was mourning she said it was for Pino's soul. Pino thought once, only once, of giving in to Valda. Then he recalled what his father had told him, '*Fare bella figura*—make a fine show but keep your face. You must have respect. Respect for who you are, for what you do, before anyone else. A man holds his head high but keeps his feet on the ground. That is why good shoes are important, so the feet are firm but comfortable on the ground. So the body can be upright and he can keep face.'

During the day, Pino talked to himself and his children, and began renovating the church. He made the stone interior resemble a cellar and varnished the wooden beams. When they could, Vincenzo, Dominic and Pasquale came and helped him. Only Pasquale still worked on the building site. Vincenzo owned his own concreting company and Dominic had a small tiling business that specialised in imported marble tiles from Carrera. They helped Pino paint and sent their wives to plead with Valda to change her mind and talk to Pino. Carmella even accused Valda of being unchristian, 'Pino is only doing this so you can get ahead in life, so you will have something for your children. It's unchristian for a wife not to help her husband.' She regretted these words the moment they were out her mouth for Valda let Carmella know that *she* knew what was Christian and what wasn't and having a restaurant in a church definitely did not pass the Christianity test.

Valda called to Vincenzo, 'Take your wife home. Your good Christian wife,' she emphasised. 'You never know, being around me may corrupt her.'

'Valda please,' Carmella pleaded, 'I didn't mean you were unchristian only you weren't behaving in a very Christian way ...'

'I know what you meant, thank you.' Valda crossed her arms. 'Now go before I forget any more Christian teachings and punch you in the nose.'

That night, when Pino arrived home from the guesthouse Valda was still awake. She was on her knees fingering her rosary and as he walked in she called out loudly, 'Dear God, I will help Pino any way I can, wash dishes, serve customers, this is my duty to him. But it is also my duty that I save his soul. A restaurant in a church is wrong, and I will pray and do penance for him. I do this only because I love him. Amen.

'And God, one more thing, please, tell him the wood trims he started painting today? In the restaurant? I don't like the colour. He should change it to a deep maroon colour that is warmer and makes people eat more. Thank you. Amen.'

La Montagna

Pino decorated the walls with Renaissance reprints, bunches of plastic grapes and chianti bottles. Inside the arched doorway he hung a wooden sculpture of a corpse in a coffin with the inscription, 'Drink and be merry as you look on him, for you will be the same when you are dead.'

It was a gift from Vincenzo.

Pasquale had kept watch at the building site for the huge wooden reels that had electrical cable wound on them. When they were empty he took them to Pino and the two of them made the reels into round tables. Valda sewed chequered tablecloths to cover them. Vincenzo's eldest son, Vince, was a signwriter and he painted the sign out the front, 'La Montagna' next to a sketch of a mountain.

Pino had a gala opening, where he invited all his friends and served free food and wine to thank them for their help. The menu was simple but tasty. He combined what he knew was popular at the guesthouse with some traditional Italian dishes:

Menu

Tomato soup or Minestra

Mashed Potatoes or Patate Fritte

Steak or Veal

Peas, Pumpkin or L'insalata

Pasta

Apple Pie and Gelato

He hired two brothers, Bruno and Mario Fazzalari as waiters. They were from the same region as Pino and when they came to Australia they visited him. Their father had once had a pair of shoes made by Pino's father. Bruno was short and stocky with a brisk energetic manner. 'Aaah Signori,' he'd proclaim, greeting guests as they entered and shaking their hands in both of his, 'you have a good day? The weather she's beautiful, yes?' He was always smiling. When they weren't too busy he took out the violin he kept in the kitchen and wandered around playing and singing and taking drink orders all at the same time.

Mario, his brother, was the opposite. Tall and reed thin he walked slowly and eyed the customers with distaste. He was a hopeless hypochondriac and was only remotely happy when telling of his latest ailment. 'You ready yet?' he would ask customers in a weary tone. And when an order was finally placed he had a way of raising one eyebrow and lamenting, 'So you want the fish? Eh, I knew it. I knew you would want the fish.' And he shook his head as he walked off leaving the customers doubting their choice and wondering whatever was wrong with the fish. When the fish was served and was delicious, they called Mario over and told him. But he looked all the more sorrowful if they seemed happy with their choice and just shrugged, shuffling away. His lugubrious manner became so well known that some people came deliberately just to be served by 'the gloomy waiter'.

Most of the patrons were Italians. They came in whole family groups: parents, grandparents, children, aunties, uncles, cousins. They drank and ate, swapped plates to taste each other's food, and ordered lots of bread so they could mop up the sauces. 'It's not bad,' they nodded to each other. 'Although in my region,' they would add hastily, 'we use more salt and it gives it a better flavour, but this is not bad.'

Later in the evening, Pino would come out of the kitchen and shake hands with each of his guests and the usual question was, 'Where are you from?' This would start the search for the common link. The guest would ask, 'Do you know the Bhorgeses?'

'No, but I know the Cirillos,' Pino would answer.

'How about the Di Francescos?'

Names would fly back and forth like a drunken butterfly until, 'I bet you know the Cavallaros?' Pino would ask.

'Cavallaro? Did you say Cavallaro?'

'Si, I am great friends with Pasquale. Do you know him?'

'No, but I heard of him. My wife's cousin lives next door to him.'

'No!'

'Yes.'

Then they'd slap their thigh and shake their head. '*Mamma mia*, it's a small world,' they'd say. By the end of the night the men would hug and kiss on the cheek calling '*Ciao*' loudly and dropping the formal '*Lei*' for the familiar '*Tu*'. The patrons would promise to come again and next time to bring a *cotoletta* that their *nonna* had cooked. They would give this to Pino to taste and offer him the recipe. And then they would spend the rest of the evening arguing among themselves, trying to agree on how it was cooked. One said to add salt to the meat when frying, another disagreed and said never add salt while frying because it toughened the meat. One said to pound the meat with a mallet to tenderise it, while another said never pound the meat as that caused it to bruise and affected the taste. Pino always tried these variations but rarely adopted them. He told me he followed his mamma's advice: '*Vai in piazza chiedi un po' di consiglio; poi ritorna a casa e fa' come ti pare*—Go into the square to ask advice; and then go home and please yourself.'

The non-Italians who ate at La Montagna were people who stared at the menu searching desperately for the obligatory steak. Bruno coaxed them to try something else, veal perhaps? It was very similar to steak, he said, only a choicer cut, really. They tried it and enjoyed it so much that they came back and ordered veal for the next three weeks until Bruno could talk them into something else.

Valda came to the restaurant on busy nights to lend a hand. She had gained a lot of weight from her pregnancies and was as wide as she was high. A barrel of a woman who scurried from table to table. She chatted to customers asking if they went to church and praying for those who didn't. She complained to whoever would listen, 'Pino, all he can do is cook but me, aaah, I work too hard all the time.' She rolled her eyes heavenwards and made a sign of the cross. 'I work like you would not believe, let me tell you.'

With so many people to talk to, in truth, she had never been happier. She went to church daily, praying for Pino's soul, and asked customers to talk to him for her. 'Eh, *scusi*,' she would say to a customer, 'could you tell my husband that Angelina (that's our eldest girl. She is home with the others, a beautiful girl too) could you tell her no-good father that she brought home the report card today and it's a very nice one. They say she's a very bright girl—like her mother, of course.'

The confused patrons would then look across the table to Pino who had heard every word, and wonder if they were really expected to repeat it. When La Montagna became so popular that people lined up outside in the hope of getting in, Pino adorned the walls with photographs of the famous people who had dined there. The Italian Ambassador, the pop star from the Saturday morning pop parade who made Angelina the envy of every girl at school when he autographed a menu for her, the soccer hero who scored the winning goal in the last five minutes of the game against Brazil. Pino kept a camera in the kitchen for such occasions and when Bruno ran into the kitchen calling, '*Mamma mia*, Pino, you will never bloody believe who we've got out there tonight,' Pino would run into the bathroom and comb his hair, rub his finger over his teeth and hand Bruno the camera. He then went out and welcomed whoever it was and asked if they would mind having their photograph taken. He stood next to them with his arm around their shoulders and Bruno told them to say *formaggio* as he snapped the picture.

When the last customers had gone Pino sat alone and poured himself a glass of *grappa* and sang words from songs of long ago.

La Montagna was officially closed on Sundays and Mondays but every Monday Pino let a group of Italian pensioners come in while he planned the week's menu and ordered the food. The pensioners played cards and the loser had to buy the coffee and wine and biscuits for the others. Most of the time he did not charge them, for he enjoyed having them near, watching them stir their coffee and drink it down in two gulps, lukewarm and bittersweet.

Caffè espresso only

People talk about coffee like it was some passing phase. I hear them all the time at La Montagna. They order cappuccino after a meal, a flat white, a long black, *caffè latte*, *macchiato—beh!* these are film star drinks and have nothing to do with real *caffè*.

The one true *caffè* is espresso—made in a three part coffee maker with a strainer in the middle. Fill the bottom part with fresh cold water. Put 3–4 (depending on how many coffees you are making) generous teaspoons of freshly ground coffee in the strainer. A blend of arabica and robusta beans is best—do not grind them too finely but so they are a little coarse. Put on the stove until all the water has risen through the centre spout and is in the top part. Do not overcook. When the last drop spits through the spout remove immediately from the heat. Pour into small cups, add two sugars and stir well.

The *caffè* should be black but with an amber coloured foam on top. Drink it in one or two mouthfuls. Never sip *caffè*—it indicates a weak constitution.

People today spend more time saying what not to eat and drink than they do eating and drinking. They say coffee is not so good for you—I say *beh!* to them. *Caffè* stimulates the brain—just the smell of it sharpens the senses. Of course, it is like everything: too much is no good but in moderation—*Buonissimo!*

The only exception to this is that it is quite permissible to add brandy or *grappa*—but just a dash.

All the others, cappuccini, *caffè latte*, have them for breakfast, they are morning foods—never for after a meal.

PP

Pino's nostrils flare as he sniffs the coffee. 'Aaah, the smell of good coffee is as deep as the winter snows and as rich as the church.' ...

Valda has bone china coffee cups with gold rims. She keeps them in the cabinet for when guests come over. She bought them for a good price from Carmella's sister-in-law who works at David Jones ...

Judy only ever drinks instant coffee. She says the coffee Pino makes is too strong and gives her a headache. She seems to have lots of headaches whether she drinks coffee or not ...

Graziella grinds coffee beans and spinkles them on her herbs. They help the comfrey to grow ...

9

For Angela — Vegetables better than the Chinese

Antipasto   *Traditions—Christmas*
Traditions—Wedding

Judy's lemon tea arrives and I watch as she sips. Tiny sips that barely wet her burgundy lips. It is like a ritual, the small rhythmic sips. Her life is full of rituals that she has borrowed or stolen from somewhere else. In her mind, these rituals give her life meaning. She walks every morning for twenty minutes, never a minute longer because she read walking is the best form of exercise and twenty minutes is the recommended optimum time. She rests with cucumber pieces over her eyes for ten minutes every day because she read this is what Joan Collins does to freshen her eyes. She does volunteer work every Tuesday at the School for the Blind because the current Prime Minister's wife does this and recommends it as an 'uplifting action'. Judy has no motions of her own.

Traditions—Christmas

'Truth and oil always come to the surface—it is an old saying from back home,' Pino said. 'You cannot hide the beginnings, if you don't use good oil the taste will never be just so. I only use extra-virgin olive oil—the olives are gathered by hand one by one and the pickers spread white linen sheets under the trees to catch any that might fall and be bruised. The olives must never touch the ground and they must be pressed immediately.' Pino sprinkled salt over the raddichio. 'Here, take this to the table.'

It was Christmas. I hang onto the memory of it greedily. I was fifteen and after years of refusing the Portellis' invitation for us to spend the day with them, this time Judy accepted. Every year we did something different. One year we went to the beach, took a picnic hamper with cold chicken, coleslaw and potato salad and the three of us sat on the sand and ate and then packed up and went home. Anthony spent the afternoon in his workshop, Judy lay down with a headache and I watched television eating potato chips. Another year we went to the Botanic Gardens—that was as good as the beach—but the worst Christmas was when I stayed in my room.

I was given my own television that year and Judy thought I'd like to watch it so she let me eat in my bedroom. I spent the day watching the religious services, the Queen's Christmas message, 'The Walton Family's Christmas'. Ruby told me her family always ate roast turkey and steamed pudding for Christmas. Her mother started making the pudding from the first of December and poured a spoonful of brandy over it each day. She even hid coins in it until the currency changed and the new money made the pudding go off. After that she kept a box full of sixpences and each year she reused them for the pudding. I told Judy about it but she said it was old fashioned and nobody ate roasts and puddings for Christmas any more.

The year we went to the Portellis' was when Pino gave me my shoes. Pino and Valda were so pleased we would be with them for the day. 'You know you are family to us, Antonio,' Valda said. 'You must come to midnight mass and celebrate exactly as we do.' So at midnight we all trudged off to the monastery gardens which was where the service was held. Chairs were set up on the grass and an altar had been erected alongside a replica stable with porcelain figures of Mary, Joseph, shepherds and the three kings. As Father Tolmino told the story of Christmas, Michael— Vincenzo and Carmella's grandson—carried out a figure of the baby Jesus and gently placed it in the empty crib. We walked back to Pino's in the crisp night air still singing 'Silent Night'. Valda put coffee on and Pino poured cognacs for everyone. Judy even let me have one. The Doogans from next door were there and we all gave presents to each other. I gave Valda a saint light. It was a statue of Saint Anthony that flashed on and off and it came with a ten-year guarantee. Valda loved it. She cried as she hugged and kissed me. 'Is beautiful. I will keep it in the kitchen. *Grazie, bella, mille grazie.*' That was when Pino gave me a box wrapped in purple tissue with silver ribbon. It looked so beautiful I didn't want to open it. Inside were my shoes. Leopard-skin stilettos that felt and smelt divine. Judy gasped when she saw them. 'They are a bit, well ... a bit ... risqué,' she said.

'What is this word? I do not know it,' Pino asked. 'You don't like the shoes? As soon as I saw them I knew Grazia would love them. They are so beautifully made. Look.' He took one and showed it to Judy. 'Handmade, from Firenze. Maybe they are a little too old for her to wear now but later, when she is older, perhaps, that is why I buy them a bit big.'

There was wrapping paper and ribbon all over the lounge room floor. Valda had made up a bed for me in Angelina's room and Judy and Anthony slept in the spare room. When we woke late the next morning, I could smell coffee and cake. The Portellis did not eat breakfast on Christmas morning but had coffee and milk, saving their appetite for dinner. Pino could not understand how people could sit down to a hot roast in the middle of summer. He had his own traditional meal.

We all sat at the dining room table—which had been extended for the occasion and had the kitchen table added on to the end of it. Valda covered both tables in her best white linen sheets. Red and green candles were on the table and Pino had Puccini's *Turnadot* on in the background. He served home-made pasta— ravioli filled with minced chicken and parsley—and covered with a Neapolitan sauce. Crayfish, prawns, calamari and baby clams dressed with lemon juice, vinegar, oil and sprinkled with finely chopped parsley. Tossed green salads, plump Jerusalem artichokes, red peppers and home-grown tomatoes dotted with oregano. He raised his glass of wine. 'Back home we say, *Tutte le feste finiscono a tavola*—all the holidays end at the table. *Buon Natale a Tutti.*'

After each course Valda and Angelina whisked the plates away and picked crumbs from the cloth. Fresh plates were set and out came crushed sweet ices flavoured with fresh fruits and a fruit platter of pineapple, strawberries, raspberries, blueberries, cherries, sweet melon and mangoes. With the coffee came almond biscuits and *fritelle*. The women cleared the table and went to the kitchen to wash, wipe and put away, the men slumped in the lounge chairs and crossed their ankles and drifted into sleep. When the last dish had been put away we all went outside and played *bocce*. Pino turned the music up so we could still hear it but Valda yelled that all the noise was making the glasses in her cabinet shake.

I watched Anthony that day. He looked more at ease when he was a part of the crowd around the Portellis' table than anywhere else. He straightened his shoulders and smiled. That night we had a light broth for tea, with the leftovers. Pino sang along with the tenors on the record and when we left he hugged us all with tears in his eyes. Anthony called out 'Ciao' as we drove away and I thought this is what Christmas should be. In the car Anthony whistled 'Nessun Dorma' and the crease between his eyebrows smoothed away.

And then Judy spoke. 'For God's sake Anthony stop that whistling, I've got a splitting headache, all that racket, I hate going there.' And Anthony stopped whistling as Judy went on, 'You have no idea what it's like … for me,' and the tears started.

The crease cut back into Anthony's forehead as he asked his wife what was wrong. 'You have no idea what it's like for me,' Judy repeated, 'Pino is such a wonderful cook and Valda's the perfect hostess, how am I expected to compete with that? I can't ask them over for dinner, I can't cook anything as good as Pino can, or if I try he gives me advice on how I should have done it and why it has turned out wrong. So I have to sit there, knowing I can never return the hospitality, knowing they will think I am rude for not returning the hospitality …'

'Oh don't fret so, Jude, I'm sure they don't think anything of the sort …'

'How would you know?' Judy snapped back. 'You're too busy drinking and carrying on to notice. I don't want to eat there again.'

Traditions—Wedding

Angelina married Flavio when I was eighteen. She had told me for years that she'd never marry a wog and she would probably die a virgin because her parents were so strict. When I was younger, often on a Saturday afternoon Judy and I went over the Portellis' and Angelina would do our hair in the laundry.

She cut my hair short and spiky on top so my face looked rounder, fatter. She talked Judy into having a colour in her hair. 'Golden Harvest will highlight your blondeness. Come on, Aunty Judy, trust me.'

'Angelina, you're looking so grown up these days, tell me, have you got a boyfriend?' Judy asked.

'Well,' Angelina lowered her voice, Valda was in the kitchen. 'Ma doesn't know this *but* you know Darlene next door? Her boyfriend has the cutest best friend, Wally. I get hot and cold flushes just thinking about him, sometimes I can't sleep for thinking about him, he's so gorgeous, and we've got so much in common, I wouldn't be surprised if we ended up together, you know, married.' Angelina squeezed the tube of colour into the bowl. I sniffed the pong of ammonia.

'That's wonderful, Angelina, but aren't you a bit young to be thinking of marriage?'

'Oh yeah, we're not but you know, we're just so good together.'

'So are your mum and dad letting you go out now?'

'No way! You know Ma, she's so unfair. I'm not allowed to go out anywhere apart from to work or out with the family. I'm a prisoner in my own home, honestly.'

Judy looked confused. 'So where do you and Wally meet?'

'Well,' Angelina blushed. 'We don't.'

'When do you see each other?'

Angelina fumbled with the colour she was mixing. 'Well, Aunty Judy, we sort of don't, I mean, I've never actually *seen* Wally, you know, but Darlene has told me all about him and I know I'd just love him and he'd really go for me, Darlene said so.' Angelina sighed. 'You know Joe is a year younger than me and he's allowed to go anywhere until all hours of the night. Typical wogs! They let their son run wild and expect their daughter to live like a nun.'

Just then Valda came in. 'Who's a nun?' she asked.

'Me. I'm expected to live like a nun,' Angelina complained.

'Pooh, you? A nun? Aaah, I pity the convent.' She pinched my cheeks.

'Oooh, your haircut is so pretty I can see your beautiful cheeks. Have a biscuit, *bella*. Angelina, what time did you get home from your class last night?'

'Oh I don't know, it was a late class, Ma, then I missed the bus and had to walk home. Hey, guess who I saw?'

'Oh God, not the Cirillos? They will be the first to start gossiping about you being out so late at night—'

'No—'

'Oh God, not the Cavallaros?'

'No, no—'

'The Chieras, oh *Dio*.' Valda shook her hands.

'No. No Italians, Ma—'

'No Italians? *Grazie Dio, grazie*.'

'No, it was Nigel, from next door.'

'Nigel, humpft! What's he doing out so late?' Valda snorted.

'He gave me a lift home.'

'You got into the car with him? You *stupida*?'

'Come on, Ma, Nigel. Next door. If I'm not safe with him I'm not safe with anyone, he's such a fag.'

'A fag? *Come si dice*? What does this mean?'

'A fag, you know,' Angelina winked at Judy. 'He's a *finocchio*, Ma.'

'*Mamma mia*!' Valda put her hand over her mouth. 'You don't say such words. I will go to the church and light a candle for poor Nigel. He's such a nice boy, I can't believe it. A *finocchio*, oh God.

I knew this would happen. I had a dream just last night about a boy in a black car eating a chicken wing.'

'What's that got to do with Nigel?' Judy asked.

Valda sighed, 'See, even you don't understand. That boy was Nigel, he drives a black car doesn't he?'

'Well it's not black, Ma, it's more dark blue.'

'That doesn't matter it's close enough.'

I interrupted, 'Zia, I don't understand why you think a boy eating a chicken wing is Nigel.'

'You see,' Valda shook her hands and the flesh on her forearms wobbled, 'he was eating chicken. Not a home-cooked, home-grown chicken, oh no. This was a bought chicken, you know, they fill them with all the hormones that turns girls into men and boys into ...' She clasped her chest and looked at Judy. 'Judy, surely you knew this about chicken? That is why we keep our own chickens. You don't cook chickens from the shops for your family do you?'

Judy blushed. 'Well ... I ...'

'We had chicken last night, Zia,' I said.

Valda slapped her forehead and sat down.

'Mamma mia,' she sighed.

The Portellis only ever ate home-grown chickens. Unlike us. Judy bought ours from the supermarket in the frozen foods department, plucked and headless, or in sections—six drumsticks and four wings. What sort of beast has six legs and four wings? Years ago, when the children were still young Valda had heard on morning talkback that poultry farmers injected chickens with hormones to fatten them. The hormones the farmers used in the chickens were passed on through the meat and eggs. Direct links had been proven between the hormone-induced chickens and girls beginning menstruation at unusually early ages. In some cases even, boys had developed breasts. Valda was horrified—none of her boys were turning into half-women, that was for sure.

She had announced her plan one morning at breakfast. 'Russo, tell your father I want a little chook yard built at the back of the shed. We can have some chooks, five or six, and get fresh eggs. When they finish laying—we eat them.'

'Papà, Ma says she wants—'

'I heard, Russo. It's not a bad idea.' Pino thought it over. He had just sat down ready to eat. He had a small mixing bowl with coffee and broken pieces of *panetone*—bread cake—in it. 'I like it,' he said. 'It will be a way for you children to see how the land looks after us, and how we must look after the land. Always there must be a fine balance.' He mixed the *panetone* into the coffee. 'When I was a boy—'

'I want to feed them,' Russell yelled quickly.

'Oh, can't I?' Alessandro pleaded.

'Well, I bags going first.'

'What about me?' Joe joined in. 'I'm bigger than you two. You'll probably be scared of them anyway.'

'Will not.'

'Will too.'

Angelina was the only one who had been unenthusiastic. 'Oh Papà no, it will be so embarrassing. No one else in the street has chickens. Oh ...' she had wailed. 'Why me? Why do I have the most embarrassing parents in the world? Is this God's way of punishing me? Don't you think it will be totally unfair on your daughter's reputation? I've got a life too, you know! They'll squawk all night and everyone will know we have them, they'll smell, they might even be dangerous, they could get out and attack me ...' Her eyes widened. 'Attacked by killer chickens ... pecking my eyes out ...'

'*Silenzio!*' Pino thumped the table.

'Oh, you just don't understand.' Angelina ran from the room. Alessandro looked worried. 'Chickens can't really peck your eyes out. Can they?'

'No of course not, your sister she's *appassionata*.' Pino waved his hand through the air. 'Always, she likes to make the story bigger. Humpft, she's like her mother. You know.' Pino reached for Alessandro and sat him on his lap. He looked into the boy's teacup eyes. 'Back home, when I was a boy as big as you, my mother, Maria, had chickens. I would feed them every day, mix the bran and water together to make a thick paste and then scoop it onto the ground. I was a good cook even then you know and the chickens loved my food. They would peck, peck, peck eating it all.

'Aaah, but then the war came and we had no food and still every day I mix the chicken bran—but for my family to eat.'

'But Papà, what did the chickens eat?'

'We had no more chickens, *piccolino*. The soldiers ate them.'

After the coop was built behind the shed, the chickens arrived. Alessandro held his breath as he took one in his hands and felt its heart beating against his fingers. All the children, even Angelina, fought over who could feed them. They played with them, chased them around the yard, and later, as the chickens got older, gathered warm eggs from their dark musty-smelling roost. The balls of fluff grew to white giddy hens who chattered incessantly and stared with dull unblinking eyes, totally self-absorbed—all except Pelé.

Pelé was a chook of courage. Alessandro named her after Pelé the Brazilian soccer player. Pelé had black spots on her right wing and could out-run, out-jump and out-peck all the others. But most of all she had courage. On the day the Doogan's dog, Rusty, got loose and ran into the back yard, little Alessandro had been terrified. Rusty barked and snapped at him but Pelé was over the fence in an instant, literally flew the coop. She dug her sharp little beak into Rusty's tail and Rusty yelped in pain and surprise. The dog swung his tail hard but Pelé hung on and was swished from side to side. Valda went out to see what was going on. She grabbed her broom and swept it towards Rusty, shooing him away. With a final flick, Rusty sent Pelé flying, then ran back to his own yard. Alessandro ran to where Pelé lay dazed on the path. 'She saved my life, Ma,' he sobbed.

When the chickens laid no more, the children watched Valda manoeuvre her large body into the coop and grab one by the neck. She walked with it flapping and screeching while Angelina tried to block her path, crying and finally throwing herself at her mother's feet. 'Please don't kill it. Spare it for me,' she begged.

Valda looked at her kindly. '*Piccolina*, this chicken is happy to die for us to eat. We are not killing for fun, for pleasure of taking God's life, we are killing for food. The chicken will not suffer and the meat will be sweeter knowing it died for us to eat. We will honour the chicken by letting your father cook it.' With one graceful swing the axe came down. As Valda released her grasp the headless chicken twitched and ran around the back yard spurting thick red blood. Later, it was hung upside down from the clothesline to bleed on the grass. The boys whooped and ran around the yard imitating the chickens, betting which one would run the furthest. Valda worked steadily and it was only when she went in for Pelé, the last chicken, that she paused. Alessandro was in a corner of the coop his arms around Pelé. Valda sniffed, 'We have enough chicken meat, it is not good to be greedy. Pelé can show the new chicks what to do.'

At school, Angelina talked to Darlene about it. 'I don't know how she does it. She loves those chickens—she mixes up special food for them and sings to them, she treats them better than she treats us and then she goes out and just murders them.'

Darlene clucked sympathetically. 'I saw on TV how this mother murdered her kids, all six of them, it was on the news. My mum says it happens to women some time. It's the ...' she lowered her voice, 'change of life. Their hormones change and it makes something snap in their brains.'

'Really?'

'Would I lie, Ange?'

'Oh Darls do you know what this means? This could be the start of it, she could have some hormone imbalance and ... and ...' Angelina looked at Darlene, horrified by the thought, 'my ma might murder us all.'

It seemed the perfect solution. Angelina and Darlene decided to put Valda on the pill. That way, they could stabilise her hormones and save the family from possible death. They switched the little sugar substitutes Valda used in her coffee with the pills in Pat Doogan's underwear drawer. But when Valda happily killed the next lot of chickens six months later Angelina gave up in despair. She told Darlene, 'Hormones can't stop her, she's just a natural killer.'

The Portellis still had chickens when Angelina married. They wanted to use their own for her wedding but knew there was no way they would have enough to feed the six hundred guests. Instead they bought the chickens from Pasquale's cousin who had a chicken farm.

They hired the town hall for the reception. All the guests stood and clapped as Angelina and Flavio walked in and passed through the Arch of Love. Pino had it sent out from Sicily. It was a white plastic arch three metres high with red hearts that flashed on and off as they walked under it. The food was magnificent and everyone agreed that Pino had outdone himself this time.

A Christmas punch was served first. This was a special occasion liqueur Pino made from lemons, vodka, sugar, water and coffee beans and it took three weeks to ripen. Then came the food: marinated fresh anchovies, lamb's liver and hot peppers, rigatoni pasta with pecorino cheese and ragout sauce, veal stuffed with hard boiled eggs and prosciutto cooked in whole tomatoes, roast lamb with garlic, rosemary and crispy roast potatoes, braised chicken stuffed with veal, liver and Swiss chard, and for Angelina, vegetables better than the Chinese—a dish Pino created especially for his daughter. Dessert was *gelato di zabaglione torta di ricotta* ... and it kept on coming with coffee and cream cakes.

Valda had broken her vow of wearing black, just for the night. She said it was bad luck to have someone in mourning at a wedding. She wore a mauve floral dress and Angelina had curled her hair. I watched as she dance with Pino. There was a strong assurance about the way they held each other, backs straight, heads high. They glided across the floor, weaving effortlessly around the other couples.

They were breathtaking.

For Angelina—*Vegetables better than the Chinese*

The Chinese are very similar to the Italians in lots of ways They are hard workers, they are good cooks and use fresh ingredients, they are respectful to many traditions, for a race that is not Italian they come very close. But they are not the same. A Chinese will die for an idea whereas an Italian will make love while he thinks of one, that is the difference. Although Valda says it is because they worship the wrong God. She says if the Chinese were all Catholics, *mamma mia*, they'd be Italians!

This is for Angelina who loves vegetables best of all.

Melt quarter of a cup of butter in a heavy-based skillet (preferably one made in Italy, the Sicilians make the best skillets). Fry some garlic, onion and celery slowly. Add any other chopped vegetables and pour half a glass of wine vinegar in. Stir slowly as you hum to *Madame Butterfly* for 15 minutes. Serve with rosé or red wine. *Salute!*

PP

Pino opens the cupboard and takes out onions, celery, carrots, potatoes, leeks, cabbage and garlic. He selects his sharpest cutting knife and begins chopping. He slices, dices, juliennes. The mechanical action is soothing to him, it is familiar ...

Valda eats garlic cloves. She says they keep her clean—on the inside ...

Angelina munches a carrot stick. 'Growing up a wog is the pits. Especially the facial hair. I had more facial hair than most guys I knew. It used to freak me out until I started waxing.' ...

Graziella does not digest well. On rising she squeezes half a lemon into a glass of water and drinks the juice. Then she rubs the cut lemon onto the white puckered scar that runs down the fourth finger of her left hand. When she touches this scar a shiver ripples over her skin as she is reminded of her strength. It thrills her.

She believes drinking the lemon stimulates her digestion. If taken first thing in the morning, Graziella can eat whatever she chooses with little ill-effect. But by midday its curative powers cease and although she has tried having another lemon before her lunch it is not the same. She eats sparingly, resenting the power food has over her. For days at a time she resists, surviving only on her lemon juice, her stomach quiet.

Then, unable to resist the hunger any longer, she eats. Her stomach swells and hardens and is only relieved by blubbery farts and burps that stink of festering food. She cannot eat in public or go out within hours of eating for fear of how her body will betray her. She rarely cooks. As she grows older the range of foods her body tolerates is less. She survives on tins of easily digestible baby food and junket ...

10

Pride
sinks
gnocchi

Antipasto   *Food is like a woman's mind*
The Sun Gods

'Look. There is Alessandro. Alessandro, we are here.' Zia Valda yells and waves. I feel my face flush, Alessandro has come to see me off!

But when I see him I also see Mira, his girlfriend. I have always been half in love with Aless. We are only a couple of years apart in age and as children we spent a lot of time together. We used to cook with Zio.

Food is like a woman's mind

Alessandro and I dragged chairs next to Pino in the kitchen.

'Today we make gnocchi,' Pino said. 'First we spread flour on the board so they don't stick –but not too much otherwise they will be hard.' He sprinkled handful after handful.

I watched and worried. I felt my breath quicken. 'Shouldn't we measure how much?'

'*Beh*, to measure tells us the number, do we eat numbers? No. It is the taste, the smell, the feel. Come on, use the flour.'

Alessandro sprinkled what looked like the exact amount. I looked at my dough and wondered if I had put enough flour in. 'I'm not sure, does it look right?'

Pino looked at the lumpy dough in front of me and wrinkled his nose. '*Bella*, do you think it looks right?'

'I don't know.'

'Well, how does it feel?'

'It's sticky.'

'*Brava*. It *is* sticky. Too sticky. Close your eyes and sprinkle a bit of flour. Let your hands tell you when it's right.'

I sprinkled and mixed. I could feel the change as the dough became more pliable, not sticky just cool, like it contained moisture and if I were to wring it in both hands maybe one tear drop could be squeezed out.

Angelina walked in. Her hair was bouffant and crackly with hair spray and her eyelashes, packed thick with mascara, were like spider's legs.

Pino did not notice her as he continued to talk. 'You know,' he said, 'food is like a woman's mind—it changes from minute to minute. And that is why we love it so.'

'Oh Pa,' Angelina groaned. 'You can't say that, it's so sexist.'

Pino looked at her then. '*Madonna!* What happened to your eyes?' He looked bewildered, as if he could not find his daughter through all the hair and make-up.

Valda came in. 'Mother *Vergina!*' She blessed herself, then hit Angelina across the head, a sharp flick that barely dented her hair. 'What happened to your face? Go and wash that rubbish off now.'

'Come on, Ma, lighten up,' Angelina sulked, 'this is the twentieth century, you know.' But all the time she looked at her father who said nothing. She walked away and slammed the door to her bedroom.

Pino turned to Alessandro and I and said loudly, 'You know when Angelina was born I looked at her and she was so hairy, like a little *scimmia*.'

'Pa, I know that word, it means monkey,' Angelina called out.

Alessandro and I giggled. With her big curly hair and hairy ears there was something ape-like about Angelina.

'A beautiful monkey,' Pino called back, and Angelina came out of her room and walked over to her father. Pino hugged his daughter using his arms, not touching her with his hands because they were still covered with flour. He kissed her on the forehead. She laughed and kissed him back and I watched, reminded, that Angelina would always be Pino's little girl.

Alessandro hugs me. He smells of soap and toothpaste.

'*Ecco*, Alessandro,' Zia says, 'why you no comb your hair?'

Alessandro hugs his mother. 'Gee, I love you too, Mamma. You're always so happy to see me. I have combed my hair. I spent twenty minutes getting my hair to look like this. Women can't resist me because of this hair.' He winks at me. I feel myself blush again. Alessandro teases all the time. What he doesn't realise is that he is usually right. Women do love his hair, which is fair and curly, not blond but golden. He is a golden boy. Tanned and athletic, with green eyes and a strong jaw, full sensual lips and a magic smile. He has Pino's charm and people like to be near him. His enthusiasm is infectious and he has a way of making people believe in themselves—because he believes in them. He sees only the best in people.

He is a junior executive for an importing company but he spends all his free time down at the beach. He has always loved the water and when I was sick and went to the beach every day he usually came with me. At first, I could barely swim. Aless would help me walk to the water's edge and let the salt water wash over me. As I gained strength, I paddled a little, until I could swim alongside him and then we would come out of the water laughing, skin tingling, and lie on our towels to dry, sharing the sunshine. He told me how he used to beg his mother to let him go to the beach and how she always worried about him drowning.

The Sun Gods

Valda did not swim.

When it was hot her children, especially Alessandro, begged her to take them to the beach. 'Please Mamma, can we go? Please?' And because her love for her children was greater than her fear of the water, she relented.

She packed bags of food, olives, pickled cauliflower, salami sandwiches, grapes, bananas, bottles of lemonade and a small flask filled with Pino's wine. She made each of them carry a bag.

At the beach they had to line up and one by one she rubbed on a mixture of olive oil—to brown them—and vinegar—to toughen their skin. They stood impatiently hopping on the hot sand, embarrassed but knowing it was futile to protest. Experience had taught them that protesting only prolonged the agony. As soon as they were able, they ran into the water, dived under a wave and left a mirrory slick behind them.

Valda sat on the sand in her black dress and woollen tights and called to them to be careful. 'An-gel-eeeee-nah, *guarda, guarda*.

Jesss-eee-pee, *mamma mia!*' She wrung her hands and frowned. 'Not too deep,' she called. 'Come back!'

They came out reluctantly, embarrassed by her calls. She hugged them tightly and their bodies left a wet imprint on her black dress. Alessandro was always the last one to come out. He swam under the water more than on the surface and pretended he was a dolphin.

'Ah-lesssss-andrrrr-ooo!' Valda wailed like a fire siren. If she couldn't see him she called for God to help. 'Oh *Dio, Dio.* Help help he's gone, my *bambino* is gone!'

When he popped up from underwater she hugged him, covering his head in kisses, murmuring her thanks, '*Grazie Dio, grazie Dio.*' Then she slapped him and yelled, '*Stupido!* You stay on top of the water, *capisci?*'

Alessandro wanted to be a lifeguard. He watched them on the beach, laughing and yelling. And their names were so wonderful: Bill, Davo, Jack. They were all tall and muscular and wore red and yellow caps that flattened their heads and made their ears stick out. He begged Valda and Pino to let him join the lifesaving squad. Valda refused even to discuss it.

Alessandro spent hours in front of the mirror imagining what he would look like as a lifeguard, white zinc on his nose and lips, laughing in the sun, running, whooping into the water. He wet his curls down and pulled his ears out. Did he look Australian?

He sneaked down to the beach as often as possible, swimming out to the buoys as he'd seen them, the Sun Gods, do. He practised beach sprints and diving into the sand for imaginary flags. One day as he was practising one of the lifesavers came over.

'Hey kid, what's your name?'

Alessandro felt his heart pounding in his ears. 'Alex,' he mumbled.

'Hi, Alex. I'm Jack. I've seen you here before, you're a pretty strong swimmer for your size. How old are you?'

'Ten. Nearly eleven.'

'Ever thought about joining the club?'

Alessandro hung his head. 'My ma won't let me.'

'Is she that big fat, er, that lady who wears all black?'

'Yeah.' Alessandro felt the hot prickling in his eyes.

'You Italian?'

Alessandro nodded.

'How about if I have a word to your ma, and see if I can't change her mind?'

'It won't do any good. You don't know my ma.'

'Listen kid, you get your ma here and leave the rest to me. Hey, what's your real name?'

'Alessandro. How'd you know ...'

Jack grinned. 'Pleased to meet you, Alessandro. I'm Giacomo Mario Capaldo. But you can call me Jack.'

The next day was a scorcher, thirty-nine degrees.

'Mamma, please can we go to the beach today?'

'No, it's too hot.'

Alessandro pleaded. 'Oh come on, Mamma, paddle your feet, it will cool you off. Please? Please, *mia bella Mamma*? *Mia bellissima Mamma*?'

Valda laughed. 'Oh, you cheeky boy.' She pinched his cheeks. 'Only for one hours we go.'

Alessandro threw his arms around her neck and kissed her. 'Thank you, Mamma, thank you.'

Alessandro saw Jack in the patrol tent and waved. Jack walked over.

'Hi Alex er Alessandro, is this your mamma?' Jack held out his hand, 'Signora, *piacere, io* Giacomo Capaldo eh, *scusi non parlare Italiano* very well.'

Valda looked the young man up and down and smiled. '*No, veramente parli bene*. Who's your family? Capaldo did you say?'

'Yes. My father Mario is an electrician, maybe you know him?'

'Capaldo,' Valda said thoughtfully. 'You are not the Capaldos that are the market gardeners?'

'That's my Uncle Jim, my father's brother.'

'Ah!' Valda put her hand to her heart. 'I worked at the East-End market for years. We bought zucchinis from the Capaldos.'

'What a coincidence.' Jack slapped his thigh.

By the end of the conversation Alessandro was allowed to join the Nipper squad. Jack assured Valda he would personally supervise all the activities and it would not interfere with Alessandro's school work. Valda invited Jack to dinner. They were having gnocchi.

Pride sinks gnocchi

We ate gnocchi on festive occasions, Christmas Day, Easter Sunday, All-Saint's Day.

Take 500 grams of old potatoes, *never* green ones. In November 1925, my mamma had been making gnocchi for 2 weeks and storing them in our cellar. It was Father Luciano's birthday and the whole village was coming to celebrate. Maria's gnocchi was well known and people lined up eagerly with their bowls. As the pots of water boiled, Maria put handfuls of gnocchi in. One by one the white balls of dough disappeared into the bubbles—but instead of bouncing up to the top as they usually did, they stayed on the bottom and broke into mushy pieces. Maria's gnocchi was turning into slush before her very eyes. Signora Formichella said it was because of pride.

'Maria Portelli is too proud and this has sunk her gnocchi,' she whispered. But Maria said pride lifted her closer to God and this would not have caused her gnocchi to sink, there must be another reason.

Green potatoes!

Old Man Carluccio had sold her green potatoes. She never used green potatoes again and her gnocchi never failed her again.

Boil the potatoes. Once they have softened—peel and mash while they are hot. Add one egg and flour to make a dough that is light and soft like a feather pillow. Roll into long cords and cut into pieces as long as your thumbnail. Put the pieces one at a time on the prongs of a fork and flick it off as if your finger is a little match striking the flint. Cook in boiling water and stir as you add them. When they rise, drain. Add cheese and sugo.

Bravo!

PP

Pino lifts his nose to the air. 'You are a Portelli,' he says to his grandson. 'The best there is.' He looks at the boy's cream-puff cheeks and black grape eyes—this boy will cook, he thinks to himself ...

Valda dreams of gypsies. They are colourfully dressed and have dark eyes. The queen of the gypsies calls to her. She asks Valda what gold she has to offer. Valda smiles at the woman. I have more gold than all of you, she says and as she sweeps her hand behind her, Pino, Angelina, Giuseppe, Russo, Alessandro, Flavio, Christian, Simona, Grace, and Antonio all appear. This is my family, she says ...

Judy looks in the mirror and squints. She can barely see her reflection. She has a mouthful of the drink that is on the dressing table. The blurred outline mirrors her action. She is cursed. That is why she is fading ...

Graziella believes in the ties of blood. Grace is linked to her by blood, they will always be together, it is like a reflection in the mirror. 'She is mine,' she whispers, 'we are blood.' ...

⟡

Alessandro has his arm around Mira. His fingers lightly stroke her arm. 'Angelina rang just before I left. She said to wish you a good trip and to say she's sorry she can't come to see you off.' Angelina is pregnant with her third child. This pregnancy hasn't gone so well for her and she has been in hospital twice already. The doctors said she must rest as much as possible. 'Rest,' she said to me. 'How can I frigging rest with two small kids?' I love Angelina but she does exaggerate everything. Zia and Zio just love their grandchildren and they have them stay every weekend. Flavio dotes on Angelina and does whatever she says. He does most of the housework and because he is a chef he does the cooking too. He has gone into partnership with Zio and is running La Montagna. Zio still cooks there, but not every night. Resting is about the one thing Angelina does—all the time.

'Ooh, you talk to Angelina? Did she say how she was feeling? We will pass by there after.' Zia looks over at Judy. 'The babies are so beautiful. Christian is three next week and so big already, and little Simona, she is so smart, she is the clever one that one.' Judy gives one of her fake smiles.

Zio looks at Anthony. 'You know the babies today, they are one thousand times smarter than we were. I love all my children and I never thought I would love other children as much as my own but when I see Angelina's children—I love them so I feel my heart bursting.' He turns to me. 'Eh, when are you going to make your parents a *nonna* and *nonno*?'

Zia hits him over the head. 'Oh *Dio*, tell this silly man not to say stupid things. Grace is not even married yet, how can she think about children?'

We all laugh. Zio shrugs and winks at me.

11

To cure illness of the body and heart—Bread soup

Appetiser   *Human dust has flecks of gold*

Entree   *Mackenzie Street*

Main course   *Giggling all the way home*
Italy—Don't you just love it?

Dessert   *Ruby Baker and Giulia Mancini*

Judy hands me a packet of pills. 'They are for travelling,' she says. 'They'll help you sleep on the plane.'

I try not to laugh.

'You laugh,' Judy says, sounding offended, 'but you never know when you'll need them. You shouldn't leave these things to chance.'

It is unbelievable how like Graziella Judy has become.

Human dust has flecks of gold

Graziella didn't leave anything to chance. She browsed in chemist shops and herbal stores and kept her options open. She bought big brown bottles of elixir, glycerine-coated capsules, small vials with precious drops. She held the bottles at arm's length and squinted as she read the labels. Pseudoephedrine hydrochloride, black cohosh, codeine phosphate, white willow, acetaminophen, chlorpheniramine maleate, feverfew leaf, prickly ash.

She used her electric mixer to grind seed pods into grey dust and brushed these carefully into clean jars. She had a teat pipette and counted One, Two, Three, out aloud as she released drops into jars. 'Don't go out on cloudy nights,' she warned me. 'Anything can happen when the moon is hidden.' She crushed aspirin and mixed it with rock dust then sprinkled it onto a photograph. 'When we die our body turns to dust—not ordinary dust—there is something different about human dust, something quite remarkable,' she whispered. 'Human dust has flecks of gold.'

That night I dreamed, somewhere, in the heel of a boot, a bald man screamed.

They are calling my flight. I look at Judy but she avoids my eye. Zia cries as she hugs me to her spongy bosom. 'Oh *Dio*, be careful, *bella*. Watch out for pickpockets and don't go out in the night and don't eat pizza in Firenze, the Florentines may have beautiful art and they think they can cook but the only place for pizza is in the south. And watch the men. The Italian men, all they want is your body ...' She can't go on she is howling so loudly.

Zio is also crying. '*Ciao, bella.*' As he hugs me he whispers, '*Ti voglio bene, per sempre.*'

Anthony looks terrible. Like an atheist who is about to die and suddenly discovers there is a God. He says nothing but puts his stick arms around me and pats me on the back. I want to say something to him but can't. He clears his throat. 'Do you need ... money? Are you sure you've got enough money?' He adds lamely, 'I could send you some, you know, if you need more.' This is the umpteenth time Anthony has offered me money. It seems to be all he has to give. 'Anthony,' I say, 'I've got heaps of money. I'll be fine. But,' I go on as I hear him swallow hard, holding in all the things we never say, 'I promise I'll let you know if I do.' I catch my breath and say, 'Bye, Dad.'

I turn to Alessandro. He kisses me softly on the lips and I linger long after the kiss has finished. I see Mira frown—fuck Mira, this is my moment. I grab Aless around the neck and let myself go. His mouth is warm and soft and his jaw moves with mine. When I open my eyes and start to close my mouth it is Aless who pulls me closer and keeps the kiss going. When we finish, we both open our eyes, and step back from each other into an embarrassed silence. Zio coughs and Zia says something to no one in particular. Mira puts her arm firmly through Aless's but I notice he keeps his hands in his pockets and his eyes stay on me.

Judy puts her hands on my shoulders as if to hold me back from getting too close. She presses her cheek to mine and makes a kissing sound in the air above my shoulder. 'Have a nice time, dear,' she says. She frowns at me and looks annoyed and, for a moment, I feel guilty for putting her through this. 'Ring us when you arrive, and keep your bag with you all the time, and get a haircut while you are there, something modern.' She touches my hair gently. I am surprised by how warm her hand is, how small it feels.

'Bye, Jude.' I kiss her on the cheek and pick up my make-up bag. '*Arrivederci a tutti*,' I call, and walk through the large shiny doors that remind me of a television series I used to love as a kid called, 'Time Tunnel'—I am entering the time tunnel. I turn to wave again but the doors are already closing and I just glimpse Zio Pino before they shut. There is no going back.

On the plane I listen to the people in the seat opposite me. They are Italians, their language is fast, furious, full of inflections, and it is not just their voices, their whole bodies are involved with the conversation.

I learnt the language at school, studied books and listened to tapes. Monotone voices that said, 'Repeat after the tone, *Ecco Signora Marzella* ... [pause] *Ecco Signora Marzella* ...' I spoke in Italian a little to Zio and Zia when Judy and Anthony weren't around. Judy said it was impolite to speak another language when not everyone could understand it. My accent is terrible—I nearly failed my final exams in the oral section because of my accent. And yet, the funny part of it all, something I have never told anyone, is this—I dream in Italian. I know the language and speak it clearly and think in it and it is only when I wake that I stumble on rolled Rrrs as the language fades away and evaporates from my throat.

Maybe it is because I have a troubled spirit. Ruby told me that was why I have problems breathing, because of my troubled spirit. It makes sense really. The Ancient Greeks believed their breath was the link between the outer world and the inner. Even the word 'breath' came from meaning 'the essence of a person'. Their breath was their soul. In Latin, the word for 'spirit' came from 'respire', to breathe. When I breathe in, I bring the outside world into me; when I breathe out, I release my inner spirit.

The hostess comes along with a noisy trolley. She serves me a plastic tray covered in silver foil, at least the cutlery is stainless steel. I grip onto it, enjoying the coolness of the metal which compensates for the plastic-looking food with the gravy that doesn't move. It is roast lamb, potatoes, carrots and peas. I close my eyes and sniff but there is no smell.

I am not hungry and I don't have to eat everything any more so I push the tray away. Away is always the beginning of a journey. If you don't have somewhere or someone to go away from, you can never go anywhere. I laugh to myself thinking that sounds like something Pino would say. I close my eyes and welcome sleep.

Mackenzie Street

'That Tony Sabato, he has a nose for making money.'

That is what people said when Anthony sold his fix-it shop and bought the old house in Mackenzie Street.

Mackenzie Street was a street on the outskirts of the inner city. It was an industrial area with one residential property left, the one Anthony bought.

'How clever,' people said. 'He'll knock it down and build an office block and lease the space and make a ton of money.'

But he didn't.

Instead, he renovated the rambling two-storey house. Restored the wrought iron balustrade, replaced the roof shingles, repaired the ceilings and advertised for tenants. The rooms were small. A single bed, wardrobe with mirrored double doors, and a worn chair or two. The kitchen was a communal one that always smelt of fat. In the corner was an industrial stove, and a griller that shone as Anthony scrubbed it each week with a bottle of Coke that he swore ate through grease better than any cleaner. The toilets and showers were in blocks of four. It was Anthony who hosed the urinals and disinfected the toilets, not willing to trust anyone else with the job of keeping house for his tenants.

His tenants weren't the type of people who were seen out much. They didn't go shopping (although they must have bought things sometime), they didn't drive cars or catch buses, they weren't the type of people to mow the lawn on Sunday morning. They were the shadow people, who crept around the edges. In the day they picked through bins, or sat in the park and smoked used-stubs or rolled their own, carefully measuring each tobacco leaf. They kept everything they found: pieces of string, a paperclip on the footpath, newspapers for cold nights and less fortunate times, cans that would earn them a few bob to spend at the pub. I heard

Judy call them 'no-hopers'. I thought about that for a long time—
to live without hope. What kept them going? I watched Anthony.
He was gentle with them.

Judy complained to Anthony that they took too much of his
time and that they weren't fit for me to be around. But he would
laugh it off and tell her not to fret so. They were his tenants, it
was his job to look after them.

On Saturdays I went with him to Mackenzie Street. I counted
the money from the television meters while he checked for leaking
taps and scrubbed the kitchen. I thought it was exciting that we
knew such people. People who couldn't afford teeth, who stuttered when they talked, who 'heard things'. Like Les. He heard
voices from outer space. He tried to explain it to me once. He
said that he communicated directly through the magnetic energy
fields surrounding the earth and he wore washers on his fingers
and foil on his head because the metals were good conductors for
the messages.

And Alec the German man who was always 'disappearing'. They
said he had been a Nazi. That he couldn't sleep because he saw
burning babies each time he closed his eyes. He was a short man,
with a pained expression on his face and he didn't speak much but
when he did, he stuttered terribly, as if each word hurt him.
'He ... he ... he ...' his eyelids fluttered, 'Hello Mi ... Mi ...
Miss.' And I would nod and walk off quickly, sparing him the
agony of saying anything else.

Some of the tenants disappeared for months at a time, leaving
their belongings as well as outstanding rent. When they returned
they were shaved clean, wore a Salvo-bin suit, had polished shoes
and a sad unsmiling face and I knew they had been in the mental
hospital. When they came back they talked quietly to Anthony
about retrieving their things. And Anthony always listened and
came to some arrangement, offering them odd jobs, bringing them

home with him to do some gardening or paint the fence, so outstanding debts could be paid off.

They gave me presents. I got books from Joycey. Leather-look Reader's Digest Condensed Books, *Christianity and the Modern Man*, *The Game of Chess*, *Yoga for Over Forty*. These books had other peoples' names in them and yellowing pages that were often loose, or worse, missing.

Beryl collected wool and knitted cardigans, socks and beanies from odd scraps in shocking colours. She gave me iridescent orange socks and a cardigan in purple and green. Judy threw them in the bin and told me to wash my hands. 'You shouldn't touch their things, you don't know where they've come from,' she said.

Norm gave me out-of-date chocolates every time he saw me. 'Here yer go, nipper.' He'd wink as he handed me two boxes of Roses chocolates. They didn't notice my double chin or fat knees or widening bottom. All they saw was that I was Mr Tony's daughter, a princess.

I felt alive with the no-hopers. I could see the edge of life in their eyes, as sure and real as the early navigators who believed there was an edge to the world and if they sailed to that edge they would fall into darkness and be lost forever. Graziella told me about edges. She made me chocolate pudding once. 'I bought the packet just for you,' she said. 'Pour contents into one litre of boiling water,' she read. I watched as she used a fork to beat the brown powder into the steaming water. The powder seemed to resist the water and floated in a dry lump on the surface. She said, 'Edges dissolve. Sometimes, if you just sit still and let things settle, look behind what you think is real, you will see things differently as the edges melt away.' When I looked down into the bowl the dry brown lump had finally surrendered into a thick muddy liquid. Graziella burnt the pudding on the edges and it was still lumpy and runny in the centre but I ate it all anyway.

When I was with the no-hopers I tried to peer into their eyes and over the edge, but then Anthony would call and tell me it was time to go home.

They often rang him at home. Always when it was most inconvenient and right on meal times, or when we had planned an outing. Quiet, nervous voices asking for Mr Tony. 'Sorry to interrupt, Miss, but Joycey's brought a right sort home this time, she can't get rid of him,' or, 'Norm's in jail. He got drunk and was in a pub brawl,' or, 'Les is smashing all the light bulbs, says the magnetic fields are closing in on him. Can Mr Tony come down?'

It seemed they could do nothing without him. And he would go to them. A tall man with strong hands who could fix everything.

Giggling all the way home

The first wedding I ever went to was Vincenzo's son's. Judy said he only invited us to show off. Everything was big and flashy. Between the dance sessions the Portelli children ran and slid on their knees down the polished dance floor. They took it in turns to drag each other across. Judy told me off and made me sit at the table with the adults. 'Your dress is all dirty,' she said. When Angelina got told off, Joe and Russell stuck by their sister. 'Come on, Ma, it's not fair, all the kids are doing it.'

'Eh,' Valda shrugged and let her daughter go.

While the adults were dancing, Russell lead his brothers and sister around the tables sipping the adults' drinks. They giggled all the way home. Next day, when the four children were violently ill and complained of headaches, Pino worried that the prawns might have been off. He made them bread soup and told them that back home if ever he was sick it was what his mamma would make him. 'Even now when I think of it my mouth waters,' he said.

To cure all illnesses of the body and the heart—
Bread soup

Where I come from, bread is never thrown away. We have a saying that if you waste bread, when you die you will have to pick up the crumbs with your eyelashes before you can go to heaven.

The bread is flat, with a hole in the centre. Delicious when fresh but even better after a few weeks of drying. Break chunks of this and place it in a saucepan with one and a half tablespoons of butter. Then add 3 cups of stock, some salt and pepper and simmer until the bread thickens the liquid. The bread gives substance to the liquid, fortifies the stock as it does the body. When this is ready, eat it with some grated cheese sprinkled over it. For illnesses of the heart, lost loves and loneliness, make sure the soup is especially hot. This will not only cure your heartache but renew the fires within so new love and passion will not be far away.

   Salute!

                                                                      PP

Pino remembers the first time he had this soup was when he just had his tonsils out. He used to suffer from terrible sore throats and his papà said he needed his tonsils removed. Old Man Carluccio scraped them out with a spoon like an ice-cream scoop. It burnt his throat like a fire but that is not what he remembers. What he remembers is that he was allowed to eat as much ice-cream as he wanted and his mamma made him bread soup ...

Valda smiles and looks like a goodluck Buddha. She is telling me to tell Pino he has cut too much bread and the soup will be too thick. 'Grace,' Pino interrupts, 'tell that she-devil to get out of my kitchen, her blabbing mouth is ruining my soup. You can never gossip when making soup, it sours the flavour. That is why your Zia can't make soup, that woman can't hold her tongue for a minute.'

'Grace,' Valda purrs demurely, 'tell your Zio I am going, but remember,' she wags her finger, 'tell him a person who talks a lot is sometimes right.' ...

Judy says I eat too much bread, it will make me fat. But when I look up fat in the dictionary it says: '... the best or richest part of something'; then I remember how fat Valda is and how when I hug her she is soft and wonderful but Judy, who has always been fashionably slim, rarely hugs and when she does she feels brittle and hard ...

Graziella can't eat bread. It gives her heartburn ...

⌒

I close my eyes to rest a moment and fall into a deep, dreamless sleep. I wake full of hope. I am excited about this trip. All my life Italy has been the magical 'backome' land of Pino's stories. You could say I have been obsessed with Italy for many years.

Italy—Don't you just love it?

As a teenager I read everything I could find on Italy. I took notes and read them out to whoever would listen. 'Judy, did you know Italy has the highest tax evasion in the world?' I read on, 'Corruption among officials is so bad that a high percentage spend time in gaol at some stage.'

'So the Italians are all crooks, is that what you're telling me?'

Judy reached for her glass. She had begun to drink. It had started as a sherry before dinner while she waited for Anthony. But as she waited and he didn't arrive, she emptied her glass and refilled it until she lost count.

'No. They're not crooks, they've got style. Listen.' I drank in information about Italy while Judy got smashed. 'There is even a book on how to behave when you are arrested. It's called, *The Handbook for the Aspiring Prisoner* and it has invaluable tips such as "When the dreaded moment of arrest arrives, offer the arresting squad coffee. Have a bag packed ready but," listen to this Jude, "leave the grated parmesan cheese to throw in at the last minute— otherwise it could go mouldy." Don't you just love it?'

Judy smiled weakly at me. 'I love it,' she echoed.

In economics class when Mr Oon taught me about Keynesian theory and laws of supply and demand, I argued the Italian perspective. 'But sir, that theory doesn't always hold true. For instance, Italy increased its tobacco production *and* was subsidised for it at a time when the European Economic Community was cutting down on tobacco sales.'

'What?' Mr Oon grabbed the news clipping I was quoting from. He read how the EEC was contracted to pay the Italian tobacco producers for an increase in crop every year, even though demand had slipped back so much that only one-third of what was being paid for was actually being used. The report went on to argue that it was possible and, knowing the Italians, highly probable, that the other two-thirds of the tobacco was not even being grown, that farmers were being paid for a phantom crop that no one wanted anyway. Mr Oon handed back the clipping. 'Everyone knows the Eyetallions are all rogues,' he muttered. 'Forget them and concentrate on Australian economical policy, that's what we were discussing.'

But I folded the article carefully and put it in my pocket.

I read how the Italian Government was thinking of passing a law to ban the destruction of their national treasures such as the Colosseum and Pantheon. Until recently, people had chipped away freely at these and used the granite to renovate their bathrooms. I fantasised about Italian men. They were all rich, perpetually tanned and impeccably dressed. They raced cars, went downhill skiing or did anything that was fast and dangerous. They gave generously to the church. They married women who gossiped too much and had opinions on everything, who told them off constantly, and wore heavy gold chains and earrings. Women who offered both cheeks to be kissed. Women who took headache powders and fed their husbands laxatives (Italians consumed more of these two products than any other European country).

I gave my month's pocket money to the missions, not because of Sister Mary Philippa's stirring talk on the dreadful conditions there but because I read how generous the Italians were. When Western Samoa was hit by a cyclone the Italians sent them 7,700 cans of sardines. And when Ethiopia was drought-stricken 20,000 kilograms of coffee beans arrived—compliments of the Italians.

I told Ruby who just shrugged and pointed out that sending coffee beans to a drought area was a bit like Marie Antoinette's famous 'Let them eat cake' line. 'What sort of help is that, Grace?'

Ruby Baker and Giulia Mancini

Ruby Baker was deceptive. She was good at sneaking in and out of things. On first impression she was small but that was part of her deception. Her feet were the clue, like a skirt caught in a door. Ruby's feet were large, the feet of a much taller person, she was just hiding in a small body. She liked that she was deceptive, prided herself in being a good cheat. She was my best friend.

Ruby was one of the few people who, when we first met, hadn't asked me to repeat my name.

Grace Sabato. Why did people find it so difficult? It was spelt exactly as it was pronounced. But I was always being asked to repeat it, 'What was that?' or 'Can you spell it?' When this happened I could feel Graziella swooping over my head, casting a shadow on my face—so I pretended it didn't matter, it didn't bother me.

But it did.

'Aaah, you're Italian,' people would say and then, as if they were complimenting me, 'but you really don't look it!' Worst of all was when I was at a friend's house and met the parents for the first time.

'Mum, this is Grace Sabato.'

'Hello dear, pleased to meet you. What was your name, I didn't catch it?'

I would hold my breath as I repeated it.

'Oh. Where do you come from?'

'Glenelg.'

'No dear. I mean where do you *really* come from, what nationality are you?'

'Well, my grandparents on my father's side were from Italy—'

'Oh. You're Eyetallion! Well, you certainly don't *look* Eyetallion. My husband's got an Eyetallion chappie working for him, maybe you know him, a relative perhaps? Hang on dear and I'll find out his name. Fred? Fred? What's the name of that Eyetallion chap at work? What's that?'

I complained about it to Ruby. 'As if I'm related to every Italian in Australia, some people are so thick! Australians keep asking where I'm from and they tell me I'm Italian. But my parents don't

even speak Italian. Kath Newman's parents are from England and
they speak so badly you can hardly understand them but no one
asks where they come from. I wonder if I could speak the language would I feel differently? Zio Pino is always going on about
"back home" but isn't this my home?'

Ruby slipped a newspaper cutting to me later in biology class.
It was about a dog. A dog whose family had moved and somehow
he had been left behind. One month later, the dog appeared at
the new house, having travelled nearly 500 kilometres. There was
a photograph with the story. It showed the family—mother,
father, son and daughter—around the dog, all smiling, looking
into the camera. The dog, a skinny unremarkable creature, sat
with his tongue hanging out looking at the boy. The article said
the dog had been led home by instinct.

I liked that story and kept it in my pocket. Later, I put it in
my underwear drawer for safe-keeping.

Ruby and I used to pray together.

'Hail Mary, full of Grace. The Lord is with thee. Blessed art
thou amongst women and blessed is the fruit of thy womb Jesus
[bow head]. Holy Mary, Mother of God, pray for us sinners. Now
and at the hour of our death. Amen. Hail Mary, full of Grace. The
Lord is ...' We saved souls at lunch time. Twice a week we gave
up our lunch hour to say the rosary knowing that each completed
rosary rescued a soul from limbo. Souls that were stuck in time
and desperately wanted to get home to the Father. I thought it
seemed a little harsh that just because someone missed mass once
and then got hit by a bus—it was always a bus—they were denied
the pearly gates and sent to limbo instead. Ruby said it was because
God was a sore loser. 'He's just not used to having anyone oppose
him. He's all loving and giving as long as we do things His way.
He's a fascist.' Ruby was very political. Once I took her over to
the Portellis' and she tried to talk about religion with Valda.

But Valda said Ruby had it all wrong. 'God tests us with things we don't understand and that is when we must have faith and trust Him. Look at me,' she had said. 'Married to Pino, that mule-headed sinner all these years. Aaah, but when he cooks, I taste God's hand in the meal. That is faith.'

When Ruby and I weren't saving souls during lunch time, we sat on the far side of the oval with our skirts hitched up and baby oil smeared on to tan our legs. Ruby wrote notes for the question box.

The question box had been Sister Mary Philippa's idea. She took the health and hygiene lessons and had introduced a question box for students so if we were too embarrassed to ask something we could write it down. The questions were read out every Friday afternoon. All the questions were about sex and the class would watch maliciously as Sister Mary Philippa would begin reading and then stop, mid-sentence, face red. She would then order us all down on our knees to pray to the Blessed Virgin to forgive whoever wrote such a filthy question. The class was given a booklet called *Teenagers*, written by the Little Sisters of the Poor. Although, as Ruby said, what would a bunch of missionary nuns know about being a teenager. It contained practical advice with dos and don'ts such as, don't kiss on a first date—it's a sure way to get pregnant, and the tragic tale of Mary Frances ...

Mary Frances

Mary Frances was a good Catholic girl who always went to mass on Sunday and confession on Saturday. One night, persuaded by a so-called FRIEND Mary Frances went to a party where there were NO PARENTS. Drinking and all sorts of CARRY ON happened. Tragically, as she was walking home, Mary Frances was hit by a [you guessed it] bus and killed. In the coffin, Mary Frances was dressed in her white confirmation dress and

184

everyone said how beautiful she looked BUT they couldn't see her soul!

The Mary Frances story was often referred to at school.

After one health and hygiene class, when we had listened to the Little Sisters of the Poor's *Audio Cassette Series on Sex*, which described the male penis as looking like a forefinger, Ruby and I came up with a rating system for penises. We stared between the legs of every pair of trousers we saw and gave the bulge a mark out of ten. We did this for months, and believed it to be an accurate system (never having the chance to really test our theories) until we learned a much easier way than staring at men's crotches. It was one we could even apply to priests who hid under robes. The Adam's Apple test.

It was Giulia Mancini who told us, along with other things, that a large Adam's Apple was a sure sign of virility. Giulia Mancini had a thick husky voice and waved her hands as she spoke. She had lived in Italy for three months and was the most sophisticated person we had ever met. On free dress day, when everyone came along in red tag Levis and Golden Breed t-shirts, Giulia Mancini wore a leather (real leather from Florence) mini, with a matching fringed vest. She had pierced ears and black fuzzy hair. She told us about her time in Italy. About boys called Angelo and Gianni who rode mopeds and taught her how to do the Chinese Drawback and French kiss.

Even Ruby the unimpressible was impressed.

At the swimming carnival, when we changed in the dressing shed and self-consciously revealed Bonds singlets and Cottontails, Giulia Mancini stripped openly to a lacy black bra and satiny crimson knickers. Even Sister Mary Philippa stared. And when Giulia Mancini held up a crocheted striped bikini Sister Mary Philippa gasped and told her to cover herself decently.

'But Sister,' she protested, 'in Italy we swam with no tops on at all.'

Sister Mary Philippa gave a cry of horror and swooned and the principal, Sister Mary Matthew, caught her just in time. 'Go and get some water, Pippa,' she ordered and then she turned to Giulia Mancini. 'And you, hussy, get dressed. You will not be swimming today.'

Giulia just shrugged and muttered something in Italian. Later she told Ruby and I it was just as well, for she could not swim. 'Imagine if I took in water and one of the penguins had to revive me, eh? Oh *Dio*,' she shook her hands, 'it would ruin my reputation. To be kissed by a nun!'

When I was fifteen and started to bleed Judy had handed me a packet of sanitary napkins and a pamphlet on menstruation. 'Here, you will need these,' she had said without looking at me. But Giulia Mancini had hugged me. 'It is the curse,' she said wisely. I knew she was right. As the blood dripped from me I felt Graziella's long bony fingers squeezing me inside. It was the curse—and I was afflicted.

When the thin-plucked eyebrow look was in fashion, Giulia Mancini left hers fuzzy and thick like a newborn caterpillar. At the annual school social the girls came in rayon chemise dresses and crepe smocks in the latest granny print patterns. But Giulia Mancini wore a strapless purple silk dress which swished freely around her as if she were underwater. The boys from Marist Brothers lined up to dance with her.

'But she hasn't even plucked her eyebrows,' wailed Ruby.

I heard Sister Mary Matthew talking to Sister Mary Philippa. 'They develop faster over there,' she had said, 'it's because of the weather. The heat.' She raised her eyebrows knowingly.

Later when I told Ruby, Ruby had scoffed. 'The weather, what a crock of shit. You know what Matthew's like.'

'But Rube,' I had said, 'she should know, after all, she is a geography teacher.'

I thought Giulia Mancini was wonderful.

She went back to Italy in our final year of high school. We wrote to each other for a short while then she stopped writing and no one knew what had become of her. Ruby said she was probably married to a Mafia boss and had ten kids.

12

For good polenta keep moving

Appetiser   *The kitchen is the heart*

Entree   *Good friends, good food, and good wine*

Main course   *The Bora*
Walk with me
To honour yourself
Debit or credit?
God must be a man

Dessert   *The woman is tarragon*

Why is it when you are in an aeroplane that you have no sense of motion? I feel up and down movements, drops in air pressure that cause my stomach to leap, but there is no sense of forward or backward movement, only a timeless stillness. There is no movement within me.

I arrive in England at night. Everyone is helpful and very polite—it all seems so orderly. The signs are in several languages and are easy to follow. There are queues everywhere and I stand and wait and listen. A voice announces that it is Sunday night, seven p.m. It is a pleasant voice—it has the sound of kind brown eyes and white straight teeth. I trust it immediately and do as it tells me. I think I will like England.

For the next few days I queue and wait. England is full of treasured possessions. National treasures, state treasures, royal treasures. I plan to see them all. The order of the place is contagious and I feel that dark side of myself surfacing. I buy maps and mark out the best routes to take to get from point to point. I plan and then follow my plan and then tick off what I have done and then list what I need to do. I visit more castles and listen to the guides tell me about the Duke who built such-and-such in honour of his Duchess. One castle has four wings and a grand ballroom in two of them. There are drawing rooms, studies, libraries, conservatories, great works of art, tapestries—but I ask to see the kitchens.

The kitchen is the heart

When the Portellis' built their house it took three months longer than the others on the estate. That was because Pino imported Italian marble for the bathroom, blinds from Venice, ornate gilt furniture from Sicily. The kitchen was Pino's proudest feature and Valda filled it with every gadget that was available. An electric mix master, toaster, vitamiser, electric frypan, coffee grinder—the only feature out of place among all the modern opulence was the oak dining cabinet they had hung their salamis in to dry. Valda used it now to display her fine china coffee cups, although the porky garlicky smell never did leave the wood and after a while even seemed to permeate the china cups.

The day they moved in Valda prayed aloud, 'Oh God, you give us this beautiful home, we thank you. Please,' she took Pino's hand, 'save this man's soul, his heart is good—it's just his head that is stupid.'

Pino grimaced. He knew Valda was happy and this was her way of telling him. He knew his children were excited about the house, about having their own rooms and a back yard. But ... he felt like a tourist who wanders and sightsees and takes in all the scenes knowing it is only transitory, that it will pass, and one day he will leave and return to the familiar, to home. This was not, would never be, his home. He could not share their joy.

The house next door was owned by an English couple, Pat and Terry Doogan, who had two children. On the day the Portellis moved in they invited the Doogans over to look at their house. When Pat commented on what a beautiful big kitchen it was, Pino shrugged and tried to look modest. 'The kitchen is like the heart. If the kitchen works well the rest of the house will be well. But if the kitchen is sick ... eh, is no good. Come, sit and we celebrate our new house and our new friends. Valda, bring some almond biscuits and wine. You know, back home we have a saying, "Friendships made in the kitchen taste the best".'

It was Pat, or Petty as Valda called her, who opened Valda's eyes to the finer things in life. Pat took Valda to have her first perm, introduced her to soap operas and talkback radio. It was Pat who taught Valda how to smoke. The two of them would have a cup of coffee together when the children had gone off to school. They sat at the kitchen table and smoked and chatted. The only thing Valda would not let Pat change about her was the colour of her clothes. She was in mourning she told Pat and would wear black until the day she died. Often she talked about her life in Italy. 'You know, Petty, I was engaged to a boy in Italy, Claudio Moroni, he was a good one with the girls, you know what I mean?'

Pat nodded, 'Too right I do love, I knew a couple like that. What happened to him?'

'I come to Australia and never went back. I married Pino.'

'Ooh, he might still be waiting for you! You better tell Pino to watch out, if he's not good to you you'll run away with your Eyetallion boyfriend.' She winked at Valda.

'Petty, let me tell you,' said Valda wagging her finger, 'Pino's all right, he's got his faults but ... well ...' Valda giggled, 'you know his nose is not the only thing big about him!'

And Pat shrieked with laughter, pretending to be shocked.

When the warm days began turning crisp as the last rays of sunshine reached the earth, Pino invited Anthony and Terry and his son Nigel to bottle wine with him. Six a.m. Sunday morning the men and the boys were out in the shed. The grapes had been fermenting in the barrels for nearly four months. By early afternoon they had all had a turn of siphoning the wine into the bottles, sometimes drinking more than actually got into the bottle. By the end of the day the yard smelt of sweet fermented grapes and even Peppi the cat was drunk. When they finished they sat under the walnut tree while Valda fussed, setting a red chequered tablecloth out with platters of salami, warm *panini* rolls, cheese, olives and roasted chestnuts. Joe moved the small stereo speakers by the window and tried playing *Deep Purple Live* before Pino ordered it off and demanded his favourites, '*Le Donna Mobile*', '*E Lucevan le Stelle*', and Mario Lanza singing '*Ave Maria*'.

They bottled *grappa*, or firewater as Terry called it. 'Bloody hell, this'll put hairs on me old fella,' he spluttered after his first mouthful.

'Terry.' Pino poured another glass for Terry and Anthony. His eyes misted over. 'True happiness comes from doing what we learn from home. *Non è vero?*'

'Too right.' Terry nodded and threw back his head as he emptied his glass. Pino refilled the glasses.

'To home, our family, that is our honour in life.'

'Too right,' Terry repeated. They clinked their glasses together. 'Australians are not so close with their families like Italians but even they know this is true. Why do they all want their own home, a piece of land, so badly? Is not to grow food, is not for shelter, they build more rooms than they need. I tell you why. It is their home they try to build. A piece of land they call theirs that belongs to them, that they belong to ...'

Terry fell to the floor.

Pino looked at Anthony, shook his head and skolled his drink. 'Australians,' he muttered.

The winemaking became an annual event for the families. It was a rugged brew, best described by Russell as 'Pappa's Piss'. The one year it seemed it was going to have quite a smooth light flavour someone left the tap on and, at the ritualistic meal at the end of the day while they sang the old favourites, the best wine Pino, Terry and Anthony had ever made drained away into the side garden under the mandarin tree, which did exceptionally well that winter.

Good friends, good food, and good wine

It was always the same at their house. No matter what the time or how short the intended visit was to be. Visitors were greeted like royalty, offered drinks and food and left with gifts. And it couldn't be refused. To refuse meant offending them. The gifts were nothing elaborate—a home-grown tomato, a leftover cutlet, some almond biscuits—simple things given in good faith. Valda and Pat shared many a morning across the kitchen table gossiping. Pat would give a brief knock on the door and sing out: 'Yoohoo, it's only me, love.' Valda invariably would be in the bathroom on her knees with a scrubbing brush and a bucket of hot vinegary water scrubbing the floor tiles.

'Hang on, Petty, I'm coming.' She hoisted herself up on one knee and leaned heavily on the bath tub. Every day Valda scrubbed the bathroom and toilet from ceiling to floor. She filled buckets with boiling water added vinegar and scrubbed until the flesh on her forearms shook violently and beads of perspiration formed on her forehead and her breath was hard and sharp in her chest. They had two toilets but the family only ever used the one down the back. Even if it meant waiting while it was occupied no one dared use the other toilet. That was 'for visitors only'.

'You're all red in the face, Val, are you all right?'

'I been cleaning the bathroom, want a cuppa?'

Valda washed her hands and put the kettle on. She had started drinking tea instead of her normal percolated coffee because her blood pressure was high. She knew you should only drink tea when you were sick—the English had it all wrong.

'What's that smell?' Pat sniffed, 'It's like salad dressing.'

'It's the vinegar I put in the water to clean.'

'Does it work?'

'For sure, it's all my mother ever used, for everything: clothes, hair, the house, vinegar is the best.'

Pat looked at Valda in disbelief.

'I no lie to you, Petty, you should try it.'

Pat lit up a cigarette and offered one to Valda. 'Guess who I saw this morning, Val?' Pat hurried on without waiting for an answer, 'Robin Masters.'

Valda inhaled slowly on the cigarette. She'd been craving this all morning and breathed out a contented sigh. 'Who?'

'Robin Masters, remember the little mousey blonde who had the twins in Nigel and Russell's class? Jeremy and what was the other one called? Jason, that's it, Jeremy and Jason, sound like a pair of dogs don't they? Remember? She always used to make goo goo eyes at anything in trousers—even Terry! She used to come to school for the twins in a little pink mini-skirt that didn't cover much, said she learnt ice-skating in the day. Remember? We thought it was strange, a grown woman going ice-skating, really!'

Valda sat back and sipped her tea between puffs. Yuk, she thought, who could drink this piss water? No wonder the English cooked so badly, if this was their national drink. 'She was a skinny little thing, no bum or bosom?'

'Well ... I wouldn't say *no* bosom.' Pat sat up straight and pushed her chest out slightly.

'Mmm,' Valda nodded, continuing, 'she looked like Angela Buffani.'

'Who's she?'

'You know, the woman who used to sing in the choir in the front row with the very high voice and then she got the cancer and had a breast off. Her voice was never the same.'

'Oh Angie, I remember her, poor little thing. She doesn't come to choir any more, I wonder what happened to her? I did hear she'd gone back to work.'

'With only one breast? *Mamma mia.*'

'Well, that's what I heard. Mind you, poor Angie probably needed the cash. I think her husband was a bit tight with money, you know, old Don.'

'Don, I no remember him.'

'Yes you do, love, the one with the mean lips.'

'Oh, the little tight mouth like a mouse's bum.'

'Well, yes, now that you put it that way, yes, I see your point.'

'So,' Valda lit up another cigarette, 'what about him?'

'Who, love?'

'Don Buffani, what did you want to tell me about him?'

'Oh.' Pat looked thoughtful, 'To tell you the truth I can't remember. I can't think what I was going to say about him.'

Pat shrugged and smiled, they sipped their tea in silence.

Valda was in shock. It was nearly midnight when she had heard the tap tapping on the bedroom window. 'Val, love, it's only me,' Pat had called. For the first time Valda realised that her friend only had pencilled eyebrows that were obviously washed off every night. It gave Pat a wide-eyed, startled look. And as she stood in her dressing gown, hair in curlers and face shining from her nightly ritual of Oil of Ulan, Valda thought, not for the first time, how ugly Australian women were. Patty was her friend and she loved her but God, Pino was lucky to have a real woman like herself! One with real eyebrows and curves. She wondered what would have happened to the Italian painters if they had been born in Australia and understood why Australians painted gum trees.

'I just remembered what I had to tell you today. Remember Robin Masters, the little blonde who *said* she went ice-skating?'

'*Si*, yes.'

'Well, I saw her in Foodland today, by the frozen peas and ... she's left her husband!'

'No!'

'And—wait for it Val—she's left the twins too. She's shacked up with her ice-skating teacher.'

'No!'

Pat nodded triumphantly.

'See, I knew there was something going on, I mean, a grown woman ice-skating—in the day, really.'

Valda gasped. Skinny little Robin Masters, with no bosoms and probably no eyebrows, who would ever have thought it?

The Doogan's daughter Darlene was the same age as Angelina and the two girls were like sisters. Angelina envied Darlene her quiet normal house. 'You don't know what it's like,' she complained. 'My mother scrubs the floors so much our house is always wet. I don't know anyone else who has to go outside to get out of the wet. And the food we eat, it's not real food like you have. We never have casseroles, or pies, or cheese that doesn't stink.'

Darlene nodded sympathetically, she'd noticed some strange smells coming from the Portellis'. She made a mental note to ask Angelina over for dinner more often.

'And Darls, we never go to the football like your family does.

My pa says footy is only for people with no brains—no offence—that soccer is the only game with any real skill.'

Angelina went to the football with the Doogans once. Mrs Doogan, who was always so polite, yelled and swore and called the umpire a mongrel and even hit a man with her umbrella because he was barracking for the other team. Darlene was embarrassed but Angelina thought it was the best time she'd ever had. 'Your mum is so with it,' she sighed. 'I bet she even wears roll-ons!'

The two girls smoked behind the shed.

'When I grow up I'm going to marry John Smith,' Angelina said.

'Who's he?' Darlene asked, thinking she didn't know any John Smith.

'I don't know yet but it's his name I want. A normal name, one people can spell. God, I hate being a wog.'

'Oh Ange, you're not a wog, I mean, not a real one. You don't smell. And you wash your hair.'

'Thanks, Darlene,' Angelina said gratefully. 'You're the best.' And then she would break off a piece of fennel for them both to chew because the aniseed taste hid the smoke smell on their breath.

There is no fennel in my vegetables in England. The food is so bland that as soon as I swallow I don't remember what I have just eaten. I am hungry all the time. I start to keep a list of what I have eaten so I can remind myself if I have had a meal or not. I sit in a pub one day and make myself think about the food. I order a ploughman's platter. I cut a piece of cheese and chew twenty times before I swallow. I am still hungry.

And I am cold.

The sky is so grey that I feel cold all the time. I shake in the castles and cathedrals and think my blood has frozen in my veins. The final straw comes when a gas pipe bursts in the building where I am staying and there is no heating for four days. I sleep with all my clothes on—shirts, jumpers, every pair of socks I packed—not bothering to wash them but rotating them in the order of which pair is next to my skin. I think of the *Bora*.

The Bora

Pino told Alessandro and me the story of the *Bora* many times. He said back home in winter it was bitterly cold.

'The wind was called the *Bora* and it came creeping, creeping like a little mouse, sniffing here and sniffing there, twitching its nose. In winter, as we slept, creep, creep the winds came and grew. The mothers called their children in, their eyes wide with fear. The shutters were locked and the houses were dark and ready for the *Bora*. My mother told me that the *Bora* was an old woman whose children had been stolen from her and with her children gone, her heart froze and she searched for them with icy fingers. When the old woman was particularly unhappy she wailed a terrible howl that came from deep inside her and echoed through the empty street. Only the sun could help her. She waited for the sun, howling every day, howling every night, and when, at last, the sun heard her and came back, a single ray pierced her chest and melted her heart and each day light leaked into her heart until all her rage quietened and she left as she had come, creeping, creeping.'

I dream of the *Bora*. I see a tall woman with white flowing hair and blue eyes reaching for me with icy fingers.

I wake rasping for breath.

I am frozen into motion and book a ferry-crossing to France. When I arrive I am charmed immediately by the sing-song language. People swear at me all the time, I cross the road in the wrong places and annoy the shopkeepers by trying to speak French. They hate me. They are so possessive about their language that no one else is allowed to use their words. But even when they are abusing me it sounds so beautiful that I cannot possibly take offence.

I am so close now I can smell it. Whiffs of Italy float by on balmy nights. But still I hesitate. I tease myself and go on to Switzerland where the Alps loom over me and look so like a post-card that I doubt their reality. I often do that—doubt what seems real, and then the smallest detail will anchor itself to fact so I know not to doubt. Like a speckle on a man's cheek.

Walk with me

Anthony had already driven away. I knocked, but no one came to the door which puzzled me. Graziella was expecting me—in fact usually she opened the door even before I knocked. I walked away, lost in thought, and found myself cutting through the park. I heard a muffled groan, like someone dying, and ran in the direction of the noise (my heart was beating—don't go, don't go, but I ignored it). I huddled behind the Morton Bay fig. Graziella was not far away standing over a park bench, her skirt raised. There was a man lying on the bench, his eyes were closed and he was moaning. Graziella held her skirt to each side like she was part of a parlour dance. She kicked the sleeping man hard in the groin.

He moaned again. Graziella looked around and I pushed against the tree, praying she could not see me.

Graziella lowered her face so it was level with the man's. I watched, horrified, thinking she was going to kiss him but she didn't. Instead, she spat on his face. I closed my eyes. When I opened them Graziella was gone.

I ran back to Graziella's house. This time I knocked only once. Graziella opened the door and smiled. 'Grace, you're late.'

'No I'm not, I came before, but you weren't here.'

'Of course I was here, I was expecting you.' Graziella walked down the passage. 'Come, I will get my other shoes, I thought we could go for a walk.'

'I don't want to walk.'

Graziella turned and stared, her eyes boring into me like sharpened steel.

'Don't want to walk? Why not? I thought we'd go over to the park.' I bit my lip and walked with Graziella.

She walked a lot. In summer she walked early in the morning before the sun's sting was at its strongest. She hated the sun. Her pale skin burnt easily and she dressed in loose brightly coloured caftans that covered all her flesh but were surprisingly cool. Whenever outdoors, she wore her large straw hat and looked like a mobile circus marquee. For the rest of the day she stayed inside, busying herself with embroidery and intricate cross-stitch patterns. When the sun had set and the cicadas and crickets began their evening song she went out again. She strode forward, holding a chequered men's handkerchief to her nose to filter the heavy sickly scent of jasmine. Many people were out in their gardens at this hour, watering exhausted plants, escaping the stifling heat trapped indoors.

This was the witching hour.

People who never exchanged glances were suddenly friendly, warmed by the heat of the day, kinship linked by the cool relief of darkness—except for Graziella. As she walked, head high, arms swinging, caftan floating, she looked at no one. People stared as she went by, lowering their voices to whisper to each other about the tall strange woman. Some said she was really a man, others said she was neither man nor woman ...

We walked together. Past the eucalypts, past the maples to the Morton Bay figs. The man was still lying on the bench. 'Disgusting isn't it,' Graziella said. 'Tramps lying about, they shouldn't be allowed here.'

We walked past the man and I was trembling. Perhaps I was going mad? Perhaps I had imagined that I saw Graziella here before? How do we know what we think we see is real?

We had nearly passed him when I sneaked a look at the man. He had a shiny gob of spittle on his cheek.

I see waterfalls that remind me of eating with the Portellis. Big meals with several courses, lots of dishes and cutlery. I swim in the hotel's heated pool and see the blue sky through the glass roof. Blue sky and warm water makes me think of summers, eating outside with the Portellis. Water jugs, platters of cold meat, pickled vegetables—*giardinieri*—cheeses, crusty fresh bread, ceramic plates, icy *gelati*.

I sit in an outdoor cafe and stir the froth on my coffee feeling ... feeling what? Lost? It dawns on me, I want to go home. I book the train and spend the rest of the day searching for an eating house that serves *baccalà*.

I have not had *baccalà* for years, since the party at La Montagna.

To honour yourself

The same week Ruby and I received our exam results, Les from Mackenzie Street died. At least that was the week they found his body—he had probably died a few weeks before. His body was found naked, buried beneath aluminium cans, his stomach alive with flies and maggots. He had somehow crawled into an aluminium can depot. Norm told me he thought Les was trying to escape, the voices had become too much for him. Les's brother was a local politican and he didn't want any reports of the death made public. 'The way Les was,' he said to Anthony, 'the things he believed, well … they just weren't "politically correct". No one would benefit if details got out. In fact, it could be very damaging.' He made it clear to Anthony that the tenants of Mackenzie Street were not welcome to attend the funeral. He had a lot of influence in the council over tenancy Acts and housing regulation laws and they would all do well just to forget they ever knew Les.

Anthony spoke to Norm about it.

'We can't just forget him,' Norm said. 'We are his mates, mates don't forget.' They organised their own service. Joycey made some sandwiches and Norm and Alec bought a couple of slabs. Beryl even put some teeth in, although where they had come from was a mystery to everyone. I made an effigy from foil and Anthony set up some chairs out the back of Mackenzie Street. They took up a collection and gave it to Norm to buy flowers but when he brought out red and yellow roses in the shape of a horseshoe with a sash across the middle, Joycey had a go at him. 'You mean ol' bugger. You've blown the money for the flowers and pinched this lot from the races.'

Norm looked like he was going to cry. 'Les liked the horses,' he said. 'He'd have liked these. I got them from a mate down the track for a good price, 'specially for him.'

Beryl told them all to settle down. 'Someone should say a few words, Mr Tony?'

Anthony looked uncomfortable. 'I'm not too good with words,' he said, 'but I'll give it a go.' He cleared his throat. 'To our mate Les, a bloody good mate, too.'

'Here, here,' Norm said.

'We hope you've gone to a better place. Somewhere ... peaceful ... where the voices won't bother you any more, mate. Rest well.'

'Here, here,' Norm said again. 'Charge yer glasses, you too, nipper. To Les.'

'To Les,' we all solemnly repeated and then emptied our beers.

We drank a few more and then Joycey came out in a boa scarf and sang 'Always', Norm got up and sang 'It's a Long Way to Tipperary' and Beryl lifted up her skirt to reveal a sad pair of chicken-stick legs and tap-danced on the cement path under the clothesline. The biggest surprise though, was from German Alec. He stood, heels together, right arm extended and sang out clearly, in the voice of an angel, and not stuttering once. They all clapped and cheered until they cried. I had never seen Anthony cry before and I watched the wrenching sobs that spilled from him now. It thrilled me to think my father had tears in him.

Judy tried to ignore it all except when we got home she said we were late for dinner, and, she sniffed, we had been drinking. We had macaroni and cheese that night. After dinner Judy passed me a thin white envelope. 'By the way,' she said, 'this came today, I think it's your exam results.'

I held the envelope and hesitated. I almost didn't want to open it. I had worked hard during my final year and I really wanted to do well but now I was scared to see how it had all turned out. But I had no cause for worry. I had passed everything and my marks were high enough to get me into university. 'Can I ring Zio Pino?' was my first response.

He was as excited as me. 'This is fantastic,' he said, 'I will arrange a celebration this Saturday night at the restaurant, bring your family and friends.' I asked Ruby to join us and Judy suggested it would be nice to invite Graziella along too. 'After all,' she said, 'she is family.'

When we were seated Pino called for everyone's attention. 'Tonight we celebrate a very special occasion. Grace so beautiful and so clever, has passed all her exams let us congratulate her,' and they all clapped while I felt myself blush. 'But,' Pino interrupted, 'not only does she pass her exams very well, she has received the highest marks in the whole state for her maths exam.' The applause started again. Ruby whistled.

Pino raised his glass. 'Please, raise your glasses as we toast Grace, who honours her family, her friends, but mainly she does honour to herself. For to do your best in anything shows the greatest respect to yourself, it is truly an honorable achievement. To Grace.' They all clinked glasses and cheered.

Pino stood again. 'One last thing ...' he began.

'Oh *Dio*,' Valda slapped her forehead, 'the man will make speeches all night, he loves the sound of his own voice, believe me I know—I have to listen to it all the time.'

'One last thing ...' Pino began again, glaring at Valda. 'As Bruno and Mario bring out the food I would like to add that I have prepared a very special meal for tonight so eat and enjoy. *Salute!*'

Fresh white Alba truffles cooked on embers and braised in champagne decorated with fresh flowers came out for the entree. Next was stuffed goosenecks in earthenware dishes and Jerusalem artichokes in a light vinaigrette. And the main course that they smelt long before they saw was *baccalà* with garlic, tomato and parsley.

Graziella refused to eat and sipped mineral water all night.

After the *baccalà* Pino stood with his glass in hand.

'Here we go again,' Valda said loudly.

'I have another announcement. Mario, my good loyal friend and waiter, is getting married this Saturday. To Mario, we wish you well.'

Ruby and I looked at each other. Mario was always such a depressed person, I couldn't imagine him being in love.

'Mario,' Ruby called, 'congratulations. It's wonderful news. Who's the lucky girl?'

'I don't know.' Mario came over and leaned on the table. 'Some girl my mother has picked for me. You know she went back to Italy last year? Well, she arranged it all. I have to pick them up from the airport tomorrow. I have a photo, see.'

Ruby's eyes widened and she passed the photo to me. It was of a beautiful young girl who looked not much older than me. 'She's so young, what's her name?'

'Maria. Aren't all good Italian girls called Maria?' Mario sighed. 'Why my mother had to do this I don't know. I am very happy with my life as it is now. I eat at the restaurant every night, I sleep late in the morning, in the afternoon I wash my socks, hang them out, go for a walk. I don't want a wife. She'll probably want me to be with her all the time.'

'Oh yeah, I'm sure she's just after your body,' Ruby quipped.

Mario sniffed. He took back the photo and looked at it distastefully.

'She's really very beautiful, Mario. How does she feel about all this?'

Mario shrugged. 'I don't know, I haven't spoken to her yet.'

'Oh come on.' I couldn't believe what I was hearing. 'Haven't you spoken on the telephone, or written to each other?'

'No.'

'Mario, this is the twentieth century. Arranged marriages went out with the Dark Ages. Why are you going through with this if you don't even know each other?'

'My mother has arranged it,' Mario said sadly, 'and you know my mother.'

'But you have a choice surely, what if you hate each other?'

'So? My father hated my mother.'

'Oh come on, Mario, that's the old way.'

'And the old ways are the best ways. Now, I get on with my work,' and he shuffled off.

'Unbelievable,' Ruby said. 'It's not Mario I feel sorry for it's that poor girl. Does she have any idea of what she's getting into?'

'Well, if she's already met Mario's mum and she's *still* coming over ...'

We both laughed.

When dessert came out even Graziella was tempted.

'The gorgonzola is easily digested,' Pino assured her. Dessert was a mixture of gorgonzola and mascarpone cheeses with fresh cream, cumin, chives and sweet mustard.

When we finished eating Pino clapped his hands and called to Bruno who came out with his violin. Pino took my hand and helped me up and we danced on the table top. Everyone cheered and at the end of the dance, Pino jumped down lightly and hugged me.

'Here,' he placed Judy's hand in Anthony's, 'dance with your wife.' We clapped as the music started up again. 'So, *bella*, what will you do now?'

'Well, I'd like to be an accountant. I've applied for a part-time job as a clerk and I'll go to uni.'

Pino raised his eyebrows and nodded approvingly.

'Aaah, very good.' he said. 'You know, I wanted Giuseppe to

go to university. I thought he would be a fine doctor. But he said the only bodies he wants to work on are car bodies.'

I laughed. Joe is car crazy and works at the local garage as a mechanic.

'Someone should go over and talk to your grandmother, she's sitting there all alone.' Pino pointed over to where Graziella sat.

'Not me, Zio. I only talk to her when I have to,' I whispered.

'Grazia,' Pino said, 'she is your grandmother. Besides she doesn't look so ... so ... fierce sitting over there.'

'Zio, I think you're going a bit soft. I'll keep my distance, thank you.'

Pino went over to Graziella. 'You must feel very proud of your granddaughter.'

Graziella stared at him and then softened her look. 'Yes, yes I do.'

On impulse, Pino reached for her hand as if to pull her up to dance with him but Graziella was too quick. She snatched her hand back sharply and stood over him.

'Don't even think about it, little man,' she threatened and she walked off to the toilets.

Valda was dancing with Mario at the time but she had seen the colour drain from Pino's face as Graziella spoke to him. She laughed so much she nearly wet herself.

Debit or credit?

Phone, gas, electricity, rates, rent, wages, interest, columns for expenses, columns for income. I ran my finger over the neat line I had just ruled. Columns for every aspect of life. Even the unexpected was accounted for in 'miscellaneous'. Recording the figures, tallying the totals, working out the cash flow, incomings and outgoings—it was the balance sheet that gave me the most pleasure. A row that didn't balance was a challenge as I checked, and rechecked, and cross-checked, decimal places, zeros, until I found the offending figure. It pleased me to find order in the world and reduce it to figures and columns neatly ruled off in red pen.

I saw accountancy as my way of keeping tabs on the debt. I told people it was a legacy of my Catholic background. 'Catholics are forever in debt, Jesus died for them, they owe their existence to God. It's a debt that's impossible to pay off.' I tried to laugh it off, but deep down, it worried me.

Buried in my work far away from Graziella's stare the right way was clear. It was just a matter of choosing a method and then applying it. I found a job easily in a small insurance firm in the audit department and thought I would happily stay there forever. The thrill of balancing, double digit inflation, current cost accounting, risk rated audits, the art of cross-referencing, it was perfect.

I arrived at work early and left long after everyone else had gone. The women on the switch gossiped about me, 'career woman', 'hard-faced', 'ambitious', 'Italian', they whispered disapprovingly. I wore my leopard-skin stilettos and that really got them going. The men flirted, briefly, and then grew sullen, suspicious.

Why did I work so hard?

Was I out to take their jobs?

They gave me the most tedious tasks to wear me down but I thrived on the repetition, the order.

At home, I spent hours ruling books, writing out schedules, lists of what to do with my time. Exercise, work, eat dinner, wash my hair, ring Ruby, visit Norm, I spent so much time planning every detail that often I ran out of time to actually do them. At the end of the day I checked off what had been completed and what hadn't and I carried over the debt of things I hadn't done. They were on the top of my list for the next day. It wasn't doing the things that mattered so much as the list. How it tallied up every night, debit or credit.

I think this was when I moved out of home. I don't really remember. It seemed as if one day I was living with my parents and the next I had moved out. I vaguely remember a conversation I had with Judy and Judy crying, and hugging onto Anthony, he patting her shoulder saying, 'There, there, she'll be back.'

He didn't look at me when I left, he couldn't bring his eyes to meet mine. He did reach for my hand and gave it a little squeeze. 'Do you need anything?' he mumbled. 'Money?' I wanted to hug him, I wanted him to look at me, to smile, instead I brushed off his hand and said abruptly, 'I earn enough on my own. I'll call by next weekend.'

My apartment was just big enough for one. I was too obsessive for anyone to want to share with me. Once a week I emptied every cupboard, scrubbing at non-existent dirt, re-ordering the contents according to height, colour—it became a challenge to discover a new way to link things together, to find connections between seemingly disconnected things. One week the cupboard contents were ordered by shape, tall glasses together small glasses together, small plates, large plates. Another week colour was the decider, clear glasses, patterned glasses, white plates, beige plates. Then usage—one glass with one dinner plate one bowl one cup; alphabetical order, B for butterplates, C for cups, G for glasses, P for plates, S for saucers—the combinations were endless.

I bought a car. A green VW named Martha that had a marijuana plant growing in the ashtray—not because I smoked but because I liked the symmetry of the leaves. It thrived in the ashtray as the sun through the window had a glasshouse effect. However, it was to be shortlived. I only knew two ways to drive, fast or stopped. So the plant was often hurled out from the ashtray into the back seat until one day the damage was irreparable and the plant died.

I started to run. Every morning I dragged myself out of bed before the sun had come up and climbed into my running clothes and ran. It forced my lungs open, held the monster asthma behind the door. For the first time in years I stopped taking my medication.

And then the impossible happened.

I lost weight.

It was so gradual at first I didn't think too much of it. Even before I felt it in my clothes, I felt lighter, more spacious in myself. I had room to breathe. Other people began to comment, uninhibited approval. I stopped eating altogether. I didn't feel the need for food any more. My clothes hung on me, my bones protruded and still I could not eat.

For good polenta keep moving

To cook good polenta you must stir all the time, never let the mixture sit still for one minute.

Add 2 cups of yellow cornmeal to cold water, stir to blend well and then add boiling water and salt. Cook this to Puccini's *Turnadot*. Leave it on a low heat for the last act and serve with beans.

If you feel like dancing while you are cooking that is fine as long as you keep stirring the polenta. The motion is important.

PP

Pino says he is a lost tourist. I say, 'Don't you mean lost traveller?' But he says, 'No, tourist. I am a lost tourist.' ...

Valda takes tours when she is widowed. Tours to the pokies, tours to other cities. She travels with other widows who wear black and need to keep moving ...

Graziella says emotions are just movements in our body and if we learn to sit very still we can control these movements and do without them ...

Judy cannot bear to be still and must move constantly ...

God must be a man

I ran. I nearly bumped into Zia one day, literally. She came around the corner just as I got there and we nearly collided.

'Grrruss,' she exclaimed, 'what's the matter? Is it your father? Your mother?' her eyes widened.

'No, nothing's wrong, Zia, I'm just running ...'

'Is someone chasing you?' Valda gripped my arm and peered over my shoulder.

'No, Zia, I'm just running, jogging.'

'Aaah, I heard on the wireless last week about a jogger who died, you shouldn't run it's bad for you. Are you sick? You look all red and sweaty, you're so skinny, you've lost weight.'

'Actually, I have lost a bit ...'

'Ah-huh! So, you have been sick. Not eating properly. I thought so. I'll send some *brodo* over tonight. We never see you any more ...'

'No, Zia. I'm eating fine.'

'Oh, my God, you have that disease—whatever it is, Princess Di has it too. She can't keep food in—that's why she's so ugly.'

'Ugly? She's considered quite an attractive woman by most people.'

'Bah, woman! She has no bosoms! That woman is like a stick, a little *rametto*. That's why her husband goes with the horsey lady. She looks like a horse but at least she has bosoms, eh?' Valda smiled. 'Aaah, I've shocked you, I can tell. Well, you're not a child any more you must learn these things. You know I've become a feminister?'

'A what?'

'A feminister. You know, the women who burn their bras and say *vaffanculo*—forgive me Jesus—to the men?' People were staring at Valda, who had started to shout.

I patted her on the arm, she was all red in the face. 'Zia, I think you'd better calm down. This can't be good for your blood pressure.'

Valda was panting. 'I'm okay, you're okay. You should think about becoming a feminister yourself. We women have to stick together. A woman is strong. *Mamma mia*, if men had to have the children all the families would just have one. They could only ever do it once. The woman is strong inside. A man needs the woman to lie his head on and feel safe. Humpft! You imagine lying your head on Princess Skinny, her bones would poke through your ears. Especially her husband with the such big ears.'

'Oh, Zia, you're awful.'

'Am I? Good. I been good too long. Father Tolmino said in mass just this morning that Jesus welcomes sinners and I thought all these years I've been good. Too good. I put up with Pino, I go to church, I visit the cemetery, I try to help where I can, I no gossip—ha, not like some I could tell you. I do the right thing, I no sin! and now Father Tolmino tells me God loves the sinners—

He forgives them. *Mamma mia*, God must be a man. I realise that this morning. What you think?'

All I could think was that Zia had gone crazy.

'You know Grrruss, I'm still wearing my bra. I tried not to but my bosoms they hurt but ... I'm wearing no underpants.'

'What?'

'*Si*.'

'But you can't ...'

'But I already am,' she smiled, 'and let me tell you, I didn't notice how windy it was until I took off my panties—little breezes keep swishing up my dress. It's a good day to get the washing dry. You no believe me?'

'Oh Zia, I believe you. What brought all this on, Zia?'

'Well, I was watching the television and on the afternoon show, "Days of the Beautiful People", Tyler was talking to Rosa about it. Did you know every woman should have their own organism. You know I never even heard of the organism before?'

'The organism?'

'*Si*, don't tell me you don't know about it too? Rosa didn't either. It's the little button that's in, you know, the bit down there, and when you push it you feel just like ... like ... like you're eating Pino's *maltagliati di pane con calamari e radicchio*, mmm.' Valda gave a small raptuous sigh.

When I visited Graziella I played with the food on my plate, rearranged it, nibbling the same piece over and over, Graziella seemed to grow smaller. For the first time I realised—Graziella could not make me eat. I stopped visiting her. I stopped visiting Zio and Zia too. I rang Anthony and Judy regularly so they wouldn't feel the need to see me. I knew something was wrong, that I was hurting myself but I felt like I was on a ride that couldn't be stopped.

When I collapsed at work they rang Judy and Anthony. My boss insisted I take some time off. It had been two months since I had seen anyone and the change was startling.

I was starving.

The woman is tarragon

Pino sat at the outdoor table waiting for me. He and Valda were to 'talk' to me—Anthony and Judy had gone over the night before and were desperate for help. I was sick, they said. I had lost weight, they were worried about my health.

'Oh my God,' Valda shrieked when she saw me. '*Madonna, bella*, come see Zio.' Valda opened the door and Pino turned to see me. He had not seen me for nearly a year but nothing could have prepared him for the sight before him now. I had grown and was considerably taller, but had shrunk in my body. My spine was slightly stooped, my chest concaved and my face long and gaunt. My hair was thin and dull and my eyes were flat. Pino saw in an instant that I was dying.

'Come, Grace,' he put out his arms around the hard knots of my back.

'Valda, bring us some coffee and cake. Lots of cake,' he added, 'I'm hungry.'

I tried to smile. I recognised the horror in his eyes, it was the same with my parents, yet when I saw that look in their eyes it gave me a perverse sense of satisfaction. Seeing it in Valda and Pino only made me feel sad. I wished I had flesh on my face so Valda could pinch my cheeks.

'Grace,' Pino said gravely, 'for a man to be skinny is to be weak. *Nervoso*. The brain, it scatters here it scatters there, it is never strong. You understand? But for the man to be fat is no good either, it is to be lazy, greedy. To stuff so full there is no room to breathe. No room for God.' Pino paused and wondered if he should be saying this. Anthony and Judy had said they were taking me to a psychiatrist, that I needed love and support not judgement. But when Pino saw my haunted eyes he knew this was no time for subtleties. He went on. 'For the man to be lean is the best. Like the flank of a horse with the muscles just showing. That is strength. Manhood. An upright stance, like a warrior. But a warrior needs to have love for someone so that he has the desire, the hunger to be a warrior. That is where the woman comes in, she is the tarragon. The biggest, strongest warrior is as weak as the skinny man without a pinch of tarragon.'

Pino reached across and took my hand. It was like holding the twigs he used to collect as a child for his mother to start the fire.

'The woman must never, never be skinny. To see the bones of a woman is to see death. The woman must be soft, with curves just as the man is hard. To watch the woman walk is to see water flowing downstream. This is our nature, understand?'

Just then Valda walked in balancing a tray with coffee and a plate piled with creamy *cannoli* cakes. I watched her move. The ripple of her flesh as she extended her arm. The soft movement of her belly against her skirt. I could see what Pino meant. Valda was all-life. I was ashamed of my own stick-like body, the handfuls of hair that came out in my brush. But I could not eat. Food stuck in my mouth and as hard as I chewed it did not break up and I could not swallow. Valda put the plate of cakes in front of me.

'Grrruss,' she purred, '*mangia*.'

'*Si. Mangia, bella*,' echoed Pino softly.

I took one of the cakes. A tube of crispy thin pastry filled with creamy golden custard and sprinkled with icing sugar. I took a bite and forced the mouthful down. It was good. I took another bite and another. Pino and Valda also ate. When I finished, Pino offered me another but a rising heat burnt its way up my gullet. I held my hand over my mouth.

Don't vomit here, don't vomit here.

I threw myself on the lawn, the cool clipped green lawn, as the vomit rushed from me, heaving uncontrollably, while they watched. Pino was shocked. He had never seen anything like it. Not even when old man Carluccio had eaten the plate of cockroaches. At the time he had thought they were stoned olives with bits of tarragon. The crunchiness should have immediately raised his doubts but he always was a greedy man, fat. He ate the whole plateful. That night he got sick and the doctor prescribed hot compresses for his stomach. The cockroaches had been sprayed with poison. Strega Nonna, the local midwife, burned candles at his feet and head. She said the poison was in his soul. A spirit had entered him and was trapped, he would have to retch it out.

Now here was I, looking like I walked with death, and retching as if a thousand spirits burned inside.

Pino could not watch. His shoulders hunched, his head drooped. He felt like a skinny man.

Valda ran to me and held me. She picked me up in her strong soft arms and carried me to the bedroom.

I reached for her hand. 'Help me, Zia,' I whispered, 'she's in me.'

'Who?'

'Graziella, she's in me.'

Valda looked into my eyes. I could see she believed me.

I stayed in their bed for seven days and seven nights. I have no idea where they slept. I had burning fevers and icy chills. Each hour Valda gave me a drink that was made from the sap of a willow tree mixed with lemon juice. I tossed and turned and murmured strange words.

I remember, even now.

Be Light, the voice said, Be Light.

I tried but it was so hard when my heart felt so heavy and part of me clung to the heaviness, scared to let go, wanting to be sucked down into the black abyss.

Be Light.

Images flashed by.

Light-footed, light-hearted, light-headed.

I opened my eyes and saw the black sky had no light. It comforted me momentarily. I stared out the curtains and waited for morning shadows. I waited for light. It sneaked up gradually and was more an absence of dark.

Be Light.

I wanted to answer, say, Why bother? but I didn't have the strength to fight back. Instead, I watched the darkness fade. I screwed my eyes tightly closed but the light came regardless, filtering through. Maybe the light was stronger than the dark? Could I believe that?

On the seventh day, I surprised everyone by walking into the kitchen. 'Zia, I'm hungry,' I said. 'I think I'd like to eat something.'

Valda had some chicken Pino had used to make a broth with. It was so tender it broke away with a fork and I had to use a spoon to eat it. I ate five mouthfuls and was not sick.

Valda hugged me.

'My Grrruss, *che bella*. She is gone. You will be all right now.'

It wasn't until the afternoon that they got the phone call from Anthony that Graziella was dead.

13 Maccheroni della montagna

Entree   *When I dream, I am home*

Main course *My heart is mine*

Dessert   *Malocchio, the evil eye*

When I dream, I am home

When I was ill, I stayed with the Portellis. I measured my days by mouthfuls and breaths. When these happened easily I knew I was still alive. Valda fed me spoonfuls of broth and her love stories, I swam with Alessandro, and spent time with Pino each day. He did everything as passionately as he cooked and ate. Even when he washed the dishes he put his whole being into it. He washed a dish and ran his hand over it, he even sniffed it. 'Aaah,' he would say. 'I missed a spot here.' And he would scrub away. We went for walks, strolling arm in arm, he'd gently rub his fingers over the new shoots on the tomato plants or sniff at forget-me-nots struggling to grow between the cracks in the footpath. One day we planted seedlings together. 'You know the dirt here is almost orange coloured. It is nothing like the dirt back home. The soil there is brown like rich chocolate and it smells ... alive. This earth smells dull and dry but things still grow very well.' He sniffed some soil between his fingers then crumbled it. He pressed with his finger, a little indentation and gently placed the seedling in. Then, as serious as a priest sprinkling holy water on a newly baptised baby's forehead, he sprinkled soil around the plant. He planted each seedling with the same care, the same attention. When he finished he knelt back on his haunches, looking over the row of green stalks peeping proudly through the earth. I asked him if he still thought about going home.

'When I dream, the mountains are always in the background, I am not the Pino you see now. Always, it is the younger me I see and I am home.' He patted my hand gently. 'That is the only time I can find my home now, when I dream. Australia is the country of my children, my grandchildren, but it is not my home,' he put his palm to his chest, 'in here. And Italy is not my home either, not any more. When I went back, when my parents died, things had changed. It was not as I remembered. And that makes me wonder, was it ever as I remembered? Or was it my thinking that made it seem so? Eh, who can know these things? All I know is that when I dream I am younger, the mountains are near, the air is sweet, my mamma and papà are with me.' Pino stood. He lifted his hat and wiped his forehead with his handkerchief. Then he put his hat back on. He had a particular way of doing it, letting the front fall full into his hand and then dropping his finger in the sharp indentation along the middle of the hat. He held it a whisker above his head and I caught a glint of sunlight between his head and his hat, and then he bowed his head and lowered the hat like he was gently pushing the light into his head.

My first sight of Italy is a pair of lovers, he with his hand up her jumper, their lips stuck together like Siamese twins joined at the tonsils. I watch from the train window and want to cheer. I am in 'backome' land. I see mountains scruffier, but more real than the Swiss Alps, whiz by from the train window. The porter sits in the corner smoking or sleeping for the whole trip and people jump off and on, yelling, always yelling and gesturing with their hands.

It is the Portelli family magnified one thousand times.

It is like walking down the driveway of the house you have grown up in, a feeling of familiarity that is so comfortable that it almost goes by unnoticed.

It is as natural as breathing.

Mopeds buzz along weaving through traffic ducking up onto footpaths and back onto roads. I wonder how many people die as a result of walking on the footpath? Do they have an annual footpath toll? I am actually beeped to get off the footpath and I jump onto the road. A little red Fiat screeches behind me. I throw up my hands and shout all the abuse I know, part Italian, part English, the Fiat driver shrugs and goes on, the moped driver winks and blows me a kiss.

I find the *pensione* in an old building: bed and bathroom for fifteen thousand *lire*. It is the one Pino told me about. It is owned by a friend of his, Enzo Carluccio. Enzo hugs me and kisses me on both cheeks and his wife Maria looks just like Valda. My room is not much bigger than those in Mackenzie Street. A double bed with a crucifix above the bed and a side table with a lamp. One dark wood cupboard and a window. I look out across—the world. The street is so narrow that I feel I could touch the building opposite me. It is identical to the one I am in. Pants, shirts and sheets hang over the balconies. I look to the right and see a cluster of high rises—swarming with cars and people. But it is the view to the left that brings a little cry, a lump in my throat. It is the mountain, La Montagna, watching me. Watching me watching it.

It is as I have always known it will be. I run outside and follow streets that seem to weave in circles and I stumble on the uneven cobbles. But no matter where I go I look up and it is there. The mountain dominates everything -even thinking. Whenever something happens people shrug and say, '*É la colpa della montagna.*' As if that explains everything. Like when it rained. My first week here torrents fell, drains packed up and flooded, it was the worst spring rainfall for as long as people could remember. They shook their heads and looked to the mountain and said, '*É la colpa della montagna.*'

There is a successful chaos everywhere here, a trust in life, in God.

Enzo's son, Dominic, takes me on his moped to his friend, a jeweller. I buy two gold chains and a bracelet that is made of the three golds and looks like it is woven. Dominic's friend is so pleased with the sale that he insists on taking us out and buying us drinks at the local bar. He doesn't lock the shop though. He says if he locks it people will know he isn't there and then it is highly likely that he will be robbed. It is better to leave the shop open and then people will think he must be nearby. He shrugs and smiles and expects me to agree with his logic—and the strange thing is, I do.

We drink coffee standing in a bar with tables but no stools. It is only ten thirty in the morning but I feel like I have been up for hours. The shops all open early and close over lunch time until late afternoon. It is a different world. I don't think of Australia at all. This seems the way it should be, the way it was always meant to be. I hunt out eating places. I know I am probably biased but nothing tastes quite as good as Pino's, still I eat and drink too much. Wine is so cheap I can't afford not to drink it.

I climb the mountain one morning.

I think I can see where Pino's house must have been. It is a self-service store now. There is a toll booth half-way up and an Italian sits with his feet on the counter, smoking. Prickly stubble dots his cheeks. His uniform is crumpled and a sprinkling of dark stains spatter his chest.

An American man strides into the booth and slams his hand on the counter.

The Italian looks up at him and continues puffing on his cigarette.

'You surely ain't gonna charge for me to walk up this here mountain?'

'Eh?' the Italian raises one eyebrow slightly.

'I ain't gonna pay it.' The American looks to his wife. 'Goddamned crooks! This whole country is filled with goddamned crooks.'

He slams his fist on the counter again. His wife says something very quietly.

'Aww shucks.' The American puts a handful of coins on the counter. 'Here, take your goddamned money.'

The Italian lifts his chin and shrugs slightly. 'Not enough,' he says.

'What?' the American roars.

'Not enough.' The Italian looks thoughtfully at his cigarette and then puts it between his lips and sucks noisily.

'The sign out the front says it cost five *milla lire* to climb the mountain.'

'The sign, she is wrong.' The Italian says in his throaty voice. 'It cost ten *milla lire*.'

'Ten *milla lire*!' The American turns bright red. His wife tugs gently on his sleeve and he throws the money down on the counter as he sighs loudly.

'*Grazie*,' the Italian says. Only now does he get up to take the money. The American walks out of the little office fuming, his wife turns around to glare haughtily at the Italian but he winks at her as he pockets half the money.

I walk up to the counter and count out my ten *milla lire*.

'Oh no, signorina,' he says, 'it only cost five *milla lire*.' He hands me back my change and squeezes my hand.

Near the top of the mountain there is an icy river. It falls into a pool after scraping over rocks, mist rises from the water like a spirit free at last. There is a tree. Part of the trunk juts out of the snow. I know this place. I have been here before, under that tree, next to that trunk. The snow curves there and my heels dig deep to stay upright. I know the shadow of that tree and the feel of the powdery snow at its base even though I have never seen real snow before. I stand still until the sun has moved from one side of the sky across to the other.

Then I leave.

Maccheroni della montagna

A recipe so alluring, so satisfying death could follow and you would go smiling. Cook to 'Recondita Armonia' from Tosca.

Boil water and add the taste of salt. Add 2 large potatoes each cut evenly into 6 pieces and a handful of fresh string beans or spinach. Just soften the outside and then add maccheroni. Cook until al dente. Drain well and layer the maccheroni and vegetables and cover with grated parmesan and edam cheeses. To Italians, food must be enjoyed first with the eyes and the nose and then the mouth. Melt a slab of butter in a frypan, add 3 diced garlic cloves and allow to brown until it sizzles like it is joining in the chorus of the music. Quickly pour evenly over the maccheroni and serve with a crusty bread stick and strong red wine. This is a true dish of the mountains, cow bells, blue skies, bearded Lombards wearing Alpini hats and velvet trousers tucked into long off-white socks made from natural wool spun in attics or stables.

This is a dish close to God.

PP

As Pino lies in bed he thinks he can smell garlic as it browns in sizzling butter. He wonders, perhaps it is the smell that is most important? All those years he cooked, he enjoyed the smell but didn't he think it was secondary to the taste? Maybe the smell is the most important ingredient of all? As he closes his eyes he feels he is drifting, like many years ago when he caught the boat to Australia, the rocking motion of the sea comes back to him now. He can no longer hear Valda, she was praying next to him but her voice has gone. He can no longer feel her hand or even his own body. The smell of garlic beckons him ...

Valda holds Pino's hand and prays. Little bubbles of garlic rise and she burps. Pino made *Maccheroni della montagna* last night, and just the two of them ate together outside, under the walnut tree. And now—look at him! She squeezes his hand and prays aloud, 'Oh God, don't take him.' ...

Anthony sits opposite Judy and they eat. The cutlery scrapes the plate and Anthony tries to chew quietly. He thinks he should say something, 'It's good, love.' Judy nods in appreciation. As Anthony cuts into the silverside a fly settles on the table. Judy shrieks and grabs the fly spray that is on top of the fridge. 'Cover your plate while I get that fly.' She sprays and wrinkles her nose as she picks up the dead fly in a tissue. 'Dirty thing. It's the beef. The smell attracts them.' She gives a quick spray of pine forest air freshener to cover the fly spray smell. They go on eating ...

Graziella chokes. A Kool Mint lodges in her throat and refuses to move, as stubborn as she has ever been. The moment between gasping for breath and breathing out for the last time, is her whole life. She let her last breath go and sees flashes of light. She thinks of her granddaughter, her one concession. She has an unfulfilled hunger that gnaws and groans. She would feed on the girl if she could, digest her morsel by morsel ...

I pack my things, kiss Enzo and Maria goodbye. Dominic holds my hand until my train comes.

Visiting places Pino has told me of has felt like a homecoming, maybe it is because he is like family to me. The word in Italian is *famiglia*, but my family has never felt familiar to me before. I think of the way Anthony pulls back when we hug, how Judy avoids my eyes when we speak. I think of Graziella kissing me with her thin hard lips. It is only now when I am far from them that I think of them, hear their voices, recognise them. Only now, when I am far from them that they have become familiar, *famiglia*.

I go south. I go to where Graziella was born.

From the train I watch the land change. It is drier, harsher than the north. I like travelling, I enjoy the journey, the sense of being a passenger, I let go of control and someone else is in charge. I am only here for the view.

I remember when I was younger and we sometimes went on weekend drives. I don't remember where we went or even if we did stop somewhere, but I do remember the drive. Swaying in the back seat, seeing other cars go past, houses, people walking, dogs, bicycles, trees, papers blown against a gutter. I watched Anthony's neck, thick skin folded over a gnawing collar, and his hands on the wheel. Big hands, strong hands. Judy's hair was teased and combed—it looked like a labyrinth of spiders' webs; layer upon layer under the perfume of lacquer. We drove and I was safe, cocooned in time. We drove in silence. I always thought we should have made some noise, talked more, like the Portellis did, but as I remember it now I suppose it was a comfortable silence.

As I leave things behind I see them clearer.

Graziella's home town is a remote village where they have only recently stopped using oxen to pull the ploughs. The houses are all old and peeling but inside they have microwaves, pigs, tumble driers and chooks. For three hours a day they are without water because the pipes are so bad they usually burst so the city engineers switch off the water each day to save the wear on the pipes. This procrastination seems to have worked, unexpected breakdowns only occur about once a fortnight. The people are superstitious. When I tell them who I am, even those who weren't born when Graziella lived here, know about her, La Strega. They raise their eyebrows and bless themselves but they are friendly to me, not thinking anything they say about her would offend me. Like Valda when she told me about her.

My heart is mine

Graziella met her husband for the first time when he was in a hospital bed with one eye bandaged and both legs in plaster. He eyed her up and down, swore, and then laughed until tears ran down his cheeks. She stood tall and stared. She devoted herself to caring for him, bringing him broth every day and sitting beside him reading books and learning English. The doctors were amazed by his progress.

Seven months later, Guido was sent home, walking. That night, Graziella delivered a healthy baby boy with thick curly hair and chubby cheeks—my father. Guido visited her room. 'When you have recovered you will move your things into my room. You are my wife and I expect you to behave like one.' He added almost as an afterthought, 'What is the child?'

'He is a boy,' she said haughtily. 'I will call him Anthony.'

Guido grunted and left the room.

She would not let Valda tell anyone back home about her pregnancy. She no longer answered her parents' letters. A month after Anthony's birth Guido announced at dinner, 'Tonight you sleep with me as a wife should.' She nodded and her cheeks burnt red. It was the first time Guido had spoken to her since Anthony's birth. Valda helped Graziella unpack her wedding trousseau, a calico nightgown that she herself had embroidered. Valda was young then, she thought love was always from God. She hugged Graziella but Graziella pushed her aside. 'I have no need for love,' she said.

Guido slept with a knife and took it to her in the black of night. She woke to icy sharpness at her throat. At first, she pleaded with him, thinking his cruel ways were because of her infidelity. She suffered the humiliation with an air of acceptance. But as time went on she realised Guido was a man haunted by demons. At night the demons claimed him and he became a thing of the blackness. Perhaps it was because of the accident, his brain had been damaged in some way. Sometimes she deliberately taunted him, daring him to use the knife, screaming at him so that Valda would lie in bed under her covers trembling and kissing her rosary. One night, Graziella grabbed the knife from him and sliced down her ring finger saying, 'This is the finger we link to the heart, the finger we wear rings on to show love.' She hissed, 'I sever the connection to the heart. My heart is mine and no one else's ...'

Often she woke to a taste so bitter it sent her rushing to the kitchen to drink pint after pint of milk. She recognised the taste that soured her mouth and fouled her breath ... it was the residue of love.

~~

In my grandmother's village there is a toothless old woman, Lucillia, who has taken a liking to me. She speaks a little English because her father went to America and her mother made her learn the language thinking they would go to live there one day. Her father never came back though. Between her broken English and my makeshift Italian we seem to communicate. She was one of Graziella's bridesmaids. Lucillia tells me many things. Some I believe and know to be true, others seem to be part of a fanciful legend coloured with superstitions. I give up trying to pin her down to details and enjoy the flow of the story.

Malocchio, the evil eye

The mother lights candles and offers prayers for the ugly daughter. At thirteen she is taller than her father and still growing. Her mother makes her sit with a large terracotta pot on her head in the hope that it will stop her growth—all it does is make her neck ache. She has fair hair and milky blue eyes in a village where women are dark and have eyes like pools of mud. Her mother weeps with shame every morning and demands accusingly, 'Can't you stoop a little? Bend your knees, act small? No man will ever want you.' When she is picked to lead the church procession her mother is honoured. She must carry a vial supposedly filled with saint's blood. The luck of the village depends on this blood liquefying. But the year Graziella carries it, it hardens and turns solid. All the crops die.

The father is determined she will marry and accumulates the richest dowry in the region for her. Neighbouring families with hairy sons come to visit but when they see her they turn away and whisper, 'She is not of this world.'

'A demon.'

'So pale!'

Men shudder, women cross themselves and mouth silent prayers. They say she has been touched by *malocchio*, the evil eye.

The girls in the village repeat the rumours of how she was conceived. How on that ill-fated night the moon was hidden behind clouds and her mother did not look under the bed to check if the devil was lurking and that tainted her father's seed with bad luck. The girls spit over their left shoulders when they talk about this so the bad luck will not touch them too.

The local church, San Antonio, has books in the church vestry. She reads them all. The more she learns, the more she is convinced that the God her mother calls on constantly does not exist. People make things happen, not God, people with power. Men have power, overtly, but women know secrets, mysteries of life. She is a woman who will use her power. She ignores the villagers, except for one.

He is the altar boy, Claudio Moroni. He is the same age as her but many inches shorter and plumper. His bulging frog eyes strain to see the outline of her nipples through her thick muslin blouse. She amuses herself by teasing him. Standing so close to him that he dribbles on her chest. She basks in her power over him but mistakes it for love.

Valda is betrothed to Claudio. Valda's parents are poor. They are so destitute that one winter they beg in the streets. Graziella strikes a deal with them, offers part of her dowry to help. They are overcome by her goodness, they whisper perhaps the giantess is an angel and not a demon? She knows instinctively their gratitude will be of use to her one day.

At twenty-seven she is resigned to spinsterhood but the father comes home one night flushed with success. There is a scheme supported by the government whereby Italian men who have migrated can marry girls from home by proxy. He put her name down and she has been accepted. She is to marry Guido Sabato, an Italian living in Australia. He is five years older than her and quite wealthy, owning some land with market gardens. He has recently been in a motorcycle accident and needs someone to care for him. It is unlikely he will ever walk again. She is furious at her parents' obvious delight in finally getting rid of her but controls her anger. It dawns on her that here is an opportunity to keep Claudio and his betrothed Valda apart.

She demurely accepts the marriage proposal. Her only request is that Valda accompany her as a companion. 'I may need help to nurse my husband and it would ease my heart to have my good friend with me. She could stay with me for three years then I will send her home to marry Claudio.'

Valda's parents are only too pleased to be able to do something for their benefactor. Graziella's mother offers prayers of thanks every morning. Perhaps the daughter is not cursed after all? An elaborate wedding is planned.

Church bells sing as the bride walks through the streets with her entourage of attendants. People whisper the curse has been lifted, some say it is a blessing from God, others say it is the garlic amulet her mother wears. The feasting and celebrations go on until late into the night. The parents have spared nothing—only the groom is missing. On impulse, she sends a note to Claudio to meet her in the church gardens after midnight. She confesses her love to him and begs him to return her feelings. She is going to a strange land, to a husband she has never met who is sick and crippled, she wants to know true love just once in her life. Claudio is flattered, it confirms what he has always suspected—that he is irresistible. He takes her in his arms—she is tall as a mountain, her hair falls softly around her face and those milky blue eyes and he speaks to her as no one ever has before.

'*Ti voglio bene, per sempre,*' he whispers, 'I will always love you.'

That night, her wedding night, the man who whispers 'I love you', the man who holds her, makes love to her, is not her husband.

She sneaks home in the early hours of the morning and knows she can bear whatever is to come. Later that day, as she and Valda stand on the dock ready to leave for Australia she looks for him in the crowd. He is there. The heat of passion, of love, rises from her toes to the tip of her head. Claudio hurries through the crowd. He is coming for her! She stands erect and proud, a woman loved. But he pushes past her—to Valda. She is just close enough to hear the very words of love he had spoken to her the previous night now being slurped into Valda's ear. She grabs him by the shoulders, draws herself up to her full height and spits in his face. Shocked onlookers feel the thrill up their spine and someone screams. They call on the Virgin to protect them against *malocchio* as Claudio's mother begins to wail, 'The evil one, she cursed my son!'

And she does.

She calls on an inner recess of darkness and draws strength from it, lets it seep through her and out from her and all around her. She wants Claudio to live forever, so she can torture him forever, like the myth of pecking eternally at the liver, like Jesus being given a sponge soaked in vinegar to quench his thirst. The idea of Claudio suffering feeds her hunger for revenge.

But hunger begets hunger and she is ravenous.

Lucillia takes me to the church of San Antonio and shows me the vestry and the graveyard that is surrounded by pine trees. 'To keep the souls in,' she says. The graves have rusted steel fences, like playpens, around them.

While we are there an old man, bent over and with a round gnomish face and smooth shiny head, follows me. He comes up to me when I am about to leave, puts his head down and weeps. Lucillia yells and shoos him away. She tells me to ignore him, he is the village idiot, senile, harmless. I sense he wants to talk to me and take his hand. '*Piacere*, Signore,' I say.

He looks up into my face and I see with a shock the round dark eyes, the crease between the eyebrows—it is my father's face. The old man says something that I cannot understand, the dialect is too pronounced. I look to Lucillia to translate.

'Oh, he is stupid,' she says. 'Ignore him.'

The old man is obviously distressed, insisting on something.

'But what did he say?' I repeat.

'He says he is old and he welcomes death but he is cursed with life. He says, you are the only one who can lift the curse, to free him.' She looks at me intently and I know she is not joking. She tells me the path of a curse is circular and she asks me if I understand. I think of Graziella's sour mouth, the bitterness on her face, and nod my head.

'*Ho capito*,' I say.

I put my hand on the old man's shiny head—I don't know why, it just seems right. In my best Italian I say, '*Ritorni a casa, sei stato salvato.*'

He smiles and his rheumy eyes overflow. Salt water follows the crevices of his face. He kisses my hand and thanks me, hurrying away like a frightened rabbit.

I breathe easy in my grandmother's village. I sleep well and remember my dreams. Dreams of herbal infusions, aromas, digestive maladies, old wet nurses with leaking bosoms, women wailing, screeching like cats, fat women who prayed and cursed and whispered, witches, mad men, winter, warm rosewood pews, stone—cold and hard, saints with frozen smiles, *Dominus Spiritos Santos*, an organ moaning, All-Soul's Day, girls singing for the festa dressed in white with garlands of flowers in their hair and a candle for the spirits in their hands, hard toffee biscuits made of honey and guaranteed to break your teeth, soaked *lupini* beans that popped out of their skin, the forest smell of roasting chestnuts, soggy smells of wine, people pushing and shoving, touching, kissing behind the church, holding him, the smell so sweet—I remember.

I walk early in the morning and notice how the trees of Italy are cypress and oak, dark greens, Australian trees are much lighter.

I miss the light.

I go shopping with Lucillia and cry when I find a jar of Vegemite in the supermarket. The shop owner tells me I can have the jar for free. He has had it on the shelf for many years, a tourist swapped it for something—he forgets what. 'Take it, please,' he smiles.

Lucillia cooks ragout for lunch. It is delicious but part way through the meal I sneak into my room and undo the Vegemite lid and sniff. I remember Pino saying that he grew up knowing he would leave his homeland one day. His parents thought the only future they could give him was for him to leave. But that the house a person owns, how much bread is on the table, these are things that are outside of who we are. I feel I have been outside of who I am for a long time.

That night I dream a different dream. It is one I have not had before. I am standing under a tree. The sun is shining through the branches and I look up, squinting, I open my mouth and my teeth fall out. They slip away from me as freely as tears, pearl white tears that don't dissolve.

I wake and pack my bag. I sit by the telephone, waiting for the call.

It is still early morning when it finally rings. Anthony's voice sounds near, as if he is in the next room. 'Pino is very ill,' he says. I sense he wants to say more. I can hear his breath through the phone. I imagine him standing gripping the receiver in his big hand, his chest tight, his shoulders stooped.

'He is ... he may be ... dying.' His voice trails off. I say, 'I'm coming home, Dad. Tell Pino I'm coming home, tell him to wait.'

I book a flight straight away and get to the airport early. I sit in the waiting lounge hugging my suitcase, his case, not wanting to let it go and cry. I know Pino will be gone by the time I get there, and all my life part of me will mourn that I missed the chance to say goodbye.

But I will cook *baccalà* and let the smell fill my house and waft over me.

Often.

Also available from Mandarin Paperbacks

SIMONE MONDESIR

Acquired Tastes

Madness and mayhem abound
in this dazzlingly fast and funny revenge tale
about sex, food and tabloid TV.

Vanessa and Alicia have been friends since schooldays.
But while Vanessa has become a ruthlessly ambitious TV
producer and man-eater, Alicia has settled for life as a
spinsterish academic and comfort eater.

Vanessa's career, however, will soon be in freefall
unless she can come up with a sensational new programme
idea. And when Alicia tells her about a new look on
sexual fantasy by Dr Fergus Archibald, a university
colleague of hers, Vanessa sees it as the ultimate audience
participation show.

All is going swimmingly until Vanessa and Fergus test
out one of his theories on high table at Alicia's college and
are discovered *in flagrante delicto* by Alicia herself – who
has been secretly in love with Fergus for some time. And
as Vanessa soon discovers, hell hath indeed no fury like a
woman scorned.

MARION HALLIGAN

Wishbone

The man opposite Emmanuelle Latimer caught her with his glance and said, What would you wish? She replied, without thinking, I would wish for the gift of making dangerous choices.'

Emmanuelle Latimer appears to have it all: a beautiful house, a successful husband, two clever children, a lovely face. But she longs for excitement, passion and danger . . . while her husband would like to spend more time with his family.

The night she first wears the daring silk dress in a seductive shade of ripe aubergine is the night her husband has a stroke – and everthing changes. Suddenly, what the Latimers, their household, their friends, wish for is coming true – in quite unexpected ways.

A sparkling, witty, sharp portrait of modern marriage.

'Her writing shimmers as much as the subject . . . celebrating and catching life as millions have known it' *Canberra Times*

ROBYN SISMAN

Special Relationship

Everybody has one special relationship in their lives – the one they never forget.

At university Annie and Jordan have a passionate love affair. But when Jordan returns to America, Annie marries steady, dependable Edward and settles down to family life in London.

Years later, Annie's son Tom finds a faded snapshot in his mother's old trunk. The girl in the photograph is his mother, her companion a familiar-looking stranger. And a handwritten message on the back hints at a mystery that has burned its hidden trail for the past two decades.

For Tom it will have consequences that overturn his past and his future. For Annie, it represents a secret that could destroy two marriages. And for Jordan, now running for the American presidency, it heralds a time-bomb waiting to explode.

'This book keeps you up until the small hours, and a little bit later . . . An irresistible read'
Daily Telegraph

'Jokey, absorbing, romantic . . . the work of an intelligent, witty woman who takes love with just the right degree of seriousness'
Amanda Craig, *Literary Review*

'Intelligent witty and gripping'
Maeve Haran

'A romance you can get stuck into'
Daily Mail

AMY TAN

The Joy Luck Club

'A brilliant first novel, *The Joy Luck Club* is the story of four mothers and their first-generation Chinese-American daughters; two generations of women struggling to come to terms with their cultural identity. Tan writes from the heart, cutting sharp edges with wit, wisdom and a gentle and delicate precision. Completely compelling'
Time Out

'Honest, moving and beautifully courageous'
Alice Walker

'She is both a consummate storyteller and a writer whose prose manages to be emotionally charged without a trace of sentimentality'
Sunday Times

'Pure enchantment'
Mail On Sunday

A Selected List of Fiction Available from Mandarin

While every effort is made to keep prices low, it is sometimes necessary to increase prices at short notice. Mandarin Paperbacks reserves the right to show new retail prices on covers which may differ from those previously advertised in the text or elsewhere.

The prices shown below were correct at the time of going to press.

☐ 7493 1898 8	**Lovesick**	Sally Brampton	£5.99
☐ 7493 2287 X	**The Pinprick**	Karina Cory	£5.99
☐ 7493 1983 6	**The End of the Hunt**	Thomas Flanagan	£6.99
☐ 7493 1319 6	**Air and Angels**	Susan Hill	£5.99
☐ 7493 1518 0	**The Ex-Wives**	Deborah Moggach	£5.99
☐ 7493 2014 1	**Changing Babies**	Deborah Moggach	£5.99
☐ 7493 2251 9	**Acquired Tastes**	Simone Mondesir	£5.99
☐ 7493 1906 2	**The Magistrate's Tale**	Nora Naish	£5.99
☐ 7493 1558 X	**Sunday Lunch**	Nora Naish	£5.99
☐ 7493 1559 8	**The Butterly Box**	Nora Naish	£5.99
☐ 7493 2221 7	**The Jewel in the Crown**	Paul Scott	£5.99
☐ 7493 1789 2	**Special Relationship**	Robyn Sisman	£5.99
☐ 7493 9591 5	**Hearing Voices**	A. N. Wilson	£5.99

All these books are available at your bookshop or newsagent, or can be ordered direct from the address below. Just tick the titles you want and fill in the form below.

Cash Sales Department, PO Box 5, Rushden, Northants NN10 6YX.
Fax: 01933 414047 : Phone: 01933 414000.

Please send cheque, payable to 'Reed Book Services Ltd.', or postal order for purchase price quoted and allow the following for postage and packing:

£1.00 for the first book, 50p for the second; **FREE POSTAGE AND PACKING FOR THREE BOOKS OR MORE PER ORDER.**

NAME (Block letters) ....

ADDRESS ....

....

☐ I enclose my remittance for ....

☐ I wish to pay by Access/Visa Card Number ☐☐☐☐☐☐☐☐☐☐☐☐☐☐☐☐

Expiry Date ☐☐☐☐

Signature ....

Please quote our reference: MAND